SURPR

Skye Fargo's mouth dropped open wider and wider as he listened to Josiah address his followers.

"Last night the man called Fargo joined with our own Asa. As you all know, a joining of the flesh is a joining of the spirit, an acceptance of the body is an acceptance of the faith. He has lain with our Asa and she with him and together they will be part of us."

"Now, hold a minute. I didn't bargain for this," Fargo began. But he stopped as three men led by Bartholomew appeared behind him.

"We will take your gun, Fargo," Bartholomew said, and Fargo saw the other three men held rifles. One reached down and pulled the Colt from his holster. "New members are not permitted to carry firearms."

Skye Fargo was a dead man if he tried to escape. He was a dead man if he stayed. Damned if he did, and damned if he didn't, he thought—and damned if he wasn't going to try . . .

THE TRAILSMAN 83

DEAD MAN'S FOREST

by

Jon Sharpe

A SIGNET BOOK

NEW AMERICAN LIBRARY

PUBLISHER'S NOTE

This book is a work of fiction. Names, characters, places, and incidents either are the product of the author's imagination or are used fictitiously, and any resemblance to actual persons, living or dead, events, or locales is entirely coincidental.

Copyright © 1988 by Jon Sharpe

The first chapter of this book previously appeared in *Mescalero Mask*, the eighty-second book in this series.

SIGNET TRADEMARK REG. U.S. PAT. OFF. AND FOREIGN COUNTRIES
REGISTERED TRADEMARK—MARCA REGISTRADA
HECHO EN CHICAGO, U.S.A.

SIGNET, SIGNET CLASSIC, MENTOR, ONYX, PLUME, MERIDIAN
and NAL BOOKS are published by NAL PENGUIN INC.,
1633 Broadway, New York, New York 10019

First Printing, November, 1988

1 2 3 4 5 6 7 8 9

PRINTED IN THE UNITED STATES OF AMERICA

The Trailsman

Beginnings . . . they bend the tree and they mark the man. Skye Fargo was born when he was eighteen. Terror was his midwife, vengeance his first cry. Killing spawned Skye Fargo, ruthless, cold-blooded murder. Out of the acrid smoke of gunpowder still hanging in the air, he rose, cried out a promise never forgotten.

The Trailsman, they began to call him, all across the West: searcher, scout, hunter, the man who could see where others only looked, his skills for hire but not his soul, the man who lived each day to the fullest, yet trailed each tomorrow. Skye Fargo, the Trailsman, the seeker who could take the wildness of a land and the wanting of a woman and make them his own.

*The Utah Territory, 1860,
just east of Devil's Slide,
a land where law was more shadow
than substance . . .*

1

"You know who that woman is in bed with you, mister?"

Skye Fargo frowned as he stared up at the two men standing at the foot of the bed, each pointing a Remington .44 Army revolver at him.

"Answer me, mister," the voice rasped, and Fargo blinked as the question revolved inside his head again. He turned to stare at the woman lying a few inches from him in the big bed and took in a fleshy figure, almost flabby in its voluminous nakedness. Large breasts with more size than shape, a round belly, and fatty thighs were all topped by frizzled red hair atop a wide face.

Fargo turned his face back to the two men. "No, I don't know who she is or how the hell she got there," he said. "But I sure as hell never picked her out."

"She's my wife, that's who she is, Mr. Fargo."

Fargo blinked again, fought the dull throbbing inside his head, and stared at the man. Recognition slowly slid across his mind. "You're the damn mayor, Efran Eason," he murmured.

"That's right," his accuser said. "And I could shoot you right there for having my wife in bed with you."

Fargo continued to stare at the man as he pushed himself up onto his elbows, glanced down at his own nakedness, and moved one hand toward the gun belt hanging on the bedpost.

"Keep away from that," the other man said.

Fargo's lake-blue eyes peered at him. Recognition again pushed its way slowly across his mind.

"Sheriff Sideman," Fargo muttered, and remembered the man's small, shifty eyes, his short nose, and tight mouth. Under close-cut black hair, Sheriff Sideman had the face of a man who sought a quick dollar the way a ferret seeks a mole.

"Now that we all recognize each other, you can get dressed, Fargo," the sheriff said. "I'm taking you to jail on Mayor Eason's charge."

Fargo glanced at the woman alongside him. She hadn't covered up and he smiled grimly to himself. The immodesty made its own statement and he let his eyes move over her body again. She had a purplish birthmark about the size of a copper penny on the side of her left thigh, and on her left wrist she wore a narrow bracelet with the initial S dangling from it. He'd seen that before, he frowned, or something like it. But he sure had never seen her before. He returned his eyes to the two men. Sideman stepped to the bedpost and removed the gun belt with the big Colt in it.

Skye Fargo swung his long legs over one side of the bed, the muscles of his powerful body rippling, and started to pull on clothes. He glanced at Efran Eason and back at the woman still on the bed. "What's the charge, Sheriff? Doing a good deed?" he asked.

"Don't get smart, mister," the sheriff growled. "Taking another man's wife is a hanging offense around here."

"I never saw her before and you goddamn well know it," Fargo said calmly, glancing at the woman

10

again as she rose and began to pull a slip over a more than ample rear.

"I doubt that Judge Hibbs will believe that," the sheriff said.

Fargo ignored the statement and realized that he remembered little of last night after he'd gone to the dance hall. Not because he'd drunk himself into a stupor. He'd only had one drink. He remembered that clearly enough, and he eyed the two men as they motioned him toward the door of the room with their guns. He felt the anger gathering inside him as he pulled the door open to step into a corridor, Sheriff Sideman close behind him.

"Keep walking," the sheriff said.

Fargo moved down the hallway and past the front desk of what was plainly the town hotel. When he was marched outside he saw his horse hitched there, the striking black-and-white Ovaro unmistakable, and he felt the moment of surprise. He let a grim sound escape his lips. They were being neat. They'd brought the Ovaro there just as they'd brought him to the hotel.

He had been set up, Fargo realized, starting with that single drink he'd been served at the dance hall, a drink that had obviously been doctored to drug him. He remembered little after that lone drink but putting the rest together was easy enough. The grim anger still inside him, he saw the woman leave the hotel, a shawl around her. She began to hurry away and Fargo glimpsed the narrow bracelet again, the initial dangling from it. It was still somehow familiar but he couldn't pin it down. His head was still fuzzy and throbbing, he realized; he needed more time to let the drug wear off completely before he began to put the pieces together. But the picture was slowly taking form. He glanced at Efran Eason's short figure. "Aren't you going to see the little wifey home, Mayor?" he asked.

"Of course I am," the man said. He tried to look righteously angry but succeeded only in appearing petulant. Eason was the kind of man who went through life like a toad, Fargo decided, forever ready to hop in any direction.

The sheriff prodded Fargo in the back with his Remington and he moved forward, his eyes taking in the still, dark town in the small hours of the morning. The town had a name, Hardrock, but it was a good deal more prosperous than many small towns in the territory. It had the usual dance hall and muddy main street, but it also boasted a bank, a church, and a schoolhouse at the north end of the town. Hardrock, he'd come to see in the few days he'd been there, sat in a perfect place in the northeast corner of Utah. Those journeying west passed through to avoid the Uinta Mountains and those coming down from Wyoming could pause there before going on in any direction. Its location let Hardrock serve those settlers who put down roots in the territory and those passing through to somewhere else. That allowed it to combine a certain air of respectability with the rowdy and raucous nature of most such towns. He'd even seen a converted grain shed made into a way station for, as the sign said, the followers of Brigham Young.

But Hardrock had been a good choice for Molly to make a fresh start, and it had been Molly Mason that had brought him here. He half-smiled and cast a glance at Sheriff Sideman walking close behind him. "All this shit wouldn't have anything to do with our little talk the other day, would it?" he offered.

"Not a damn thing. You were caught with Mayor Eason's wife in bed. It's as simple as that."

"The hell it is." Fargo laughed. He followed the sheriff's gesture as he motioned to a narrow building with a star on the window. Fargo opened the door and went inside, where a barred cell took up the back half of the room with a smaller cell to one side and a desk and gun cabinet in the front of the space.

The sheriff pushed him into the larger cell and slammed the door shut. Fargo turned around, grimaced as a sharp throb stabbed through his head. Sheriff Sideman surveyed him from outside the bars for a long moment.

"Of course, if you want to talk about not staying in jail, I might be able to persuade the mayor to be forgiving," the sheriff said.

Fargo allowed a slow smile. "According to him, his wife wound up in bed with me. Hell, I'm the one who ought to be forgiving." Fargo saw the sheriff's eyes harden.

"Sleep on it, Fargo. That's advice I'd take," Sheriff Sideman growled.

"Sure thing," Fargo said. He sat down on the narrow cot that took up one part of the wall. He saw a cracked, white porcelain pitcher of water and an open toilet in the other corner of the cell. He waited until the sheriff stalked from the office and slammed the front door after him before he lay back and stretched out on the cot, his long legs dangling from one end. A small smile touched his lips. Their little scheme was really very transparent but he needed to put all the pieces into place, from the very beginning. He had to be certain he was right before they came again. He closed his eyes and let his mind unwind, travel backward to when he had arrived in Hardrock. And why.

It had been only a few days back, the moment he'd finished bringing in Bill Dempster's herd. He'd taken the long, hard drive only because it ended at Hardrock and it gave him a chance to keep a promise made long ago. Molly's letters had told him she worked at the general store and she and Amy lived in a white cottage just past town. He had arrived late in the day, found the cottage and Molly.

"Oh, my God, I'm dreaming," she had gasped before flying into his arms, her lips quickly finding his.

"You look wonderful, Molly," he said when he pulled back. "As bright and sunny as always." No mere words on his part, and Molly Mason's dark hair and snapping, black-brown eyes always reflected the brightness that was inside her, a quality that saw her through trials and troubles without turning her bitter. She had taken her arms from around his neck as the little girl appeared behind her, the same dark bright eyes and deep-brown hair.

"This is an old friend, Amy," Molly introduced. "He remembers when you were born back in Kansas six years ago."

"He sure does," Fargo echoed, and drew a shy smile from little Amy. He had dinner with Molly and her daughter, and after Amy was in bed and asleep, Molly took him into her room and her lips found his again.

"I've never forgotten how you helped me after Chuck was killed," she said. "And that wonderful year after Amy was born when you'd stay with me after every trip."

"Seems long ago, doesn't it?" he had remarked.

"Too long," Molly had said. "But you've finally come and it's time to replacing dreaming with doing." She had turned her words into action as with a wriggle of her shoulder she let the nightgown drop away. Time had done nothing to diminish the lovely

14

curve of her full breasts, he saw. Their dark-pink points were already firm with desire.

He started to pull off his clothes but Molly stopped him. "Let me," she breathed, and began to undress him, pausing to caress and kiss and rub against him after each garment was pulled away. When he was finally naked, his powerfully muscled body against her, Molly Mason uttered a deep and groaning sigh as he began to make love to her. She responded with hunger and memories, everything wrapped and entwined together, as their bodies quickly melded. Molly's full curved loveliness clung to him and the clock turned back with every soft scream of her pleasure. When she rose up in climax, her thighs encased him with sweet quivering.

Later, stretched out against him, Molly nuzzled into his chest. "How long can you stay, Skye?" she asked.

"Long enough," he said. "Been on the trail too much. Came here to see you and do nothing else."

"Wonderful," Molly had murmured. "But we'll have to be a little more discreet than we used to be. I've a daughter and a job and I'm a respected member of the community."

"You call the shots, honey."

"Same time, same place tomorrow night." Molly had laughed as she wrapped one leg over his and went to sleep in his arms.

He left in the morning before little Amy awoke, and decided to pay the town barber a visit. It was when he left the barber shop that he found the two men standing beside the Ovaro.

"Fargo?" the one man said, and went on without waiting for an answer. "Been looking for you. Bill Dempster told us you rode an extra fine Ovaro. I'm Sheriff Sideman. This is our mayor, Efran Eason." Fargo nodded and felt a touch of wariness stab at him. "We've been waiting for you to arrive with Dempster's herd. He told us you were due soon." Fargo felt the wariness grow stronger inside him and waited. "We've a special job for you, Fargo," the sheriff said. "We need you to trail a man for us."

"Sorry, you'll have to get somebody else," Fargo said. "I'm tired, I'm trail-weary, and I'm taking a good long rest."

"We need the very best, and that's you. We'll pay you twice your usual fee," the mayor had said.

Fargo smiled pleasantly. "Sorry, but not this time around, gents."

"Three times your usual fee," Efran Eason offered.

"This hombre must be real important to you," Fargo commented.

"He's a very dangerous man and we want him back, dead or alive. That's why we need you," the mayor said.

"He got a name?" Fargo asked.

"Frank Tupper," the sheriff answered.

"He a specially good woodsman and mountain man?" Fargo queried.

"No, but time's very important. We need someone who can pick up the trail and catch him before he gets too far away," the sheriff put in.

"What'd he do?" Fargo asked out of curiosity.

"He cleaned out the town treasury, most of the money in the bank, and killed two tellers," Sideman answered.

"Just the same, you'll have to find somebody else, I'm afraid," Fargo said. "I don't usually turn down good money but this is a special time and a special visit here. Sorry."

"We can't accept that, Fargo," the sheriff said, his voice hardening. "This is too important to us.

We need him caught and we know you're the only man who can do it."

" 'Fraid you'll have to accept it, gents," Fargo said pleasantly. He ignored the glowering frowns as he swung onto the Ovaro. Their eyes bored into him as he rode away.

That night he returned to Molly, and once again, after Amy was asleep, she came to him with all her eager warmth, and the night became a thing of sweet touchings and throbbing tenderness until he lay with her in the warm aftermath of ecstasy. Once again, when morning came, he left before little Amy woke, and it was later in the day when Efran Eason and the sheriff approached him. He had stopped at the smithy to have the Ovaro's right foreshoe tightened and the two men appeared with a third man who joined them on horseback. Fargo took in the man in the saddle and saw sand-colored hair cut very short, a square face with a pushed-in nose, and a mouth that turned down at the corners. It was a face as harsh as a granite quarry.

"This is Olson, Fargo," Sideman said. "He's a kind of deputy for me."

"Whatever that means," Fargo remarked.

"It means he does special jobs for me when I need him," the sheriff said. Olson stared down from the saddle, his harsh face unsmiling. He had brought the horse alongside a deep water trough, Fargo saw. "We still need you on that job, Fargo," the sheriff pressed.

"The answer's still no," Fargo returned, and let the annoyance show in his voice now.

"You're obviously enjoying your visit to Hardrock," Sheriff Sideman said.

Fargo's eyes grew narrow. "What's that mean?" he questioned.

"Miss Mason is a lovely young woman, a welcome part of our community," Efran Eason said.

"You've been following me," Fargo muttered, steel coming into his voice.

"Just to be sure you don't leave town without considering our offer again," the mayor said.

"I don't like being watched. It makes me very irritable, and things happen when I get irritable," Fargo growled. "I'm not taking your damn job, so get off my back."

Olson's voice cut in, a harsh, grating sound to it. "Hell, he's more interested in tail than trail," the man said.

Fargo stood very still for a moment. When his hand lashed out, it was with the speed of a rattler's strike and he closed his fingers around Olson's belt buckle. He yanked, all the strength of his powerful shoulder muscles behind it, and Olson came forward from his horse. Fargo twisted and the man landed headfirst into the water trough with a loud and wet splash. Fargo, his grip loosened, stepped back and then forward, pushing Olson's head deeper into the water.

"Let him go. You're drowning him, dammit," he heard the sheriff say and saw the man reach for his six-gun.

"You draw and you can be sure I'll drown him," Fargo said, and the sheriff lowered his hand. Fargo waited another ten seconds and then yanked Olson up from the trough. The man came up coughing and spitting water between deep, heaving breaths. Fargo half-twisted him around in the trough and drove his forearm against the man's throat, Olson's head pressed against the edge of the trough. "Molly Mason's an old friend of mine. You call her tail again and I'll break your damn neck, you hear me?" Fargo rasped.

Olson made a gasping sound that sufficed as a yes and Fargo let him go and stepped back. He turned to Efran Eason and the sheriff while Olson lay in the trough regaining his breath, his head just above water.

"I make myself clear to you gents?" Fargo growled.

The sheriff's face showed he was a man who knew when to let caution rule over anger. Efran Eason showed only fear. He quickly turned and walked away with Sideman. Fargo waited till Olson pulled himself from the trough and led his horse away.

The smith was waiting with the Ovaro and Fargo swung onto the horse and rode from town. Eason and his sheriff were two worried and persistent men but perhaps they'd learned their lesson finally, Fargo hoped. He didn't return to Molly's place till after dark. His eyes searched the streets as he neared the cottage but he spied no shadowy figures. Once he was inside, Molly pressed her lips to his and finally pulled away, dismay wreathing her face.

"Amy's sick. She's in her room," Molly told him. "She's running a fever. I'm afraid I'll be sitting up with her through the night."

"Anything you need?" Fargo asked.

"No. I'll call Doc Grogan if she's not better, come morning," Molly said.

He cupped her face in one hand. "I'm sorry for Amy and disappointed for me," he said.

"That makes two of us," Molly said as she leaned into his chest.

"See you tomorrow night," he told her. He patted her soft bottom as she kissed him at the door, and went back into the night. He was hungry and decided a drink and something to eat would be perfect. He had walked the Ovaro to the dance hall, tethered the horse to the post outside, and gone into a round and smokey room, a curved bar taking up one side. His glance halted at the woman in the bright blue dress. She was pushing forty, he guessed. It was easy to recognize the granite-faced man beside her. Olson's eyes found him and the man turned his back to Fargo as he continued talking to the woman.

Fargo strolled to the small tables beside the wall, eased his big frame into the small, straight-backed chair, and one of the house girls in a short frock and black net stockings came over. They all wore pretty much the same outfit, he noted. The girl, still young but with too much makeup around her eyes, regarded him with a bored appraisal.

"What's your pleasure, big man?" she had said. "Pour, plate, or pillows?"

"We'll start with pour. Bourbon," he'd said, laughing, and watched her wend her way through the crowded room. Two of the other dance-hall girls crossed his line of vision and he watched them idly, one almost skinny, the other almost fat, and neither particularly pretty. The girl took a ridiculously long time to return with his bourbon, he remembered now, and she'd hurried away without another word. Not that he cared at the time. He'd been happy to relax and slowly sip the drink.

Fargo stretched his neck muscles as his thoughts clicked off. He had come to the end of his rememberings. Now he had to piece together what happened afterward, not that it was terribly hard to do. Olson had seen an opportunity to get back at him and arranged to have the bourbon doctored. Then he'd reported what he'd done to his boss. The sheriff had undoubtedly called in Efran Eason, and the rest of the scheme was cooked up. It was really quite transparent, all of it an attempt to make him agree to trail for them.

But they'd made themselves a mistake, Fargo grunted. He'd let them go through all the motions until they came to realize it wouldn't work. He let his mind wander some more and the woman who had been in the bed next to him swam into his thoughts. He frowned as he thought about the narrow bracelet with the initial dangling from it. It continued to seem familiar. Suddenly he sat up and a half-laugh, half-snort fell from his lips. The girl that had brought him the bourbon had worn one with her initial dangling from it. So had the other two girls, he recalled. It was a kind of house trademark, apparently, and Fargo smiled as he lay back on the cot. He'd been sure she hadn't been the mayor's wife, but now he knew where they'd gotten her. From the dance hall, he laughed. That explained her lack of modesty. She was used to lying naked before strangers. They had put together a neat package, Fargo pondered. There had to be another link, something yet to come to add the final finish. The judge, he laughed. They had to have a judge to complete the picture and make him think he was in deep trouble.

Fargo smiled, pushed himself up further on the cot, and closed his eyes. Sleep seemed the best idea at the moment and he turned on his side and drew slumber around him at once. The cell remained a quiet place through the night, and when daylight came in through the lone window he rose, used the porcelain pitcher of water to wash and freshen himself. He'd just finished when the front door opened.

Sheriff Sideman entered first, Efran Eason behind him, and the last figure was a tall, lanky, long-faced man with graying hair and the face of a pious, backwoods preacher. But the man wore a black frock coat, a wing collar, and a diamond stickpin in a blue cravat.

Fargo eyed the man with amusement. "You must be the judge," he said, and saw the man's pale-gray eyes widen in surprise.

"I didn't expect to be expected," the man said with a glance at Efran Eason.

"I'm good at figuring out things," Fargo remarked casually.

"I have no idea what that means, sir," the man said. "I'm Judge Warren Hibbs, and Mayor Eason asked me to stop in and explain the seriousness of the charges against you."

"That's real nice of you, Judge," Fargo said blandly.

"Forcing another man's wife to bed is a serious thing. I'd have to sentence you to hang if you're found guilty," Judge Hibbs said gravely.

"What about the mayor's good wife? It takes two to tango," Fargo remarked.

"I understand Mrs. Eason says you seized her on the street and forced her into the hotel room with you," the judge said.

"Only it was the other way around. She did the forcing," Fargo said.

"That hardly seems likely," the judge said.

"You didn't see her naked," Fargo said. "I feel sorry for the good mayor."

"Dammit, Fargo, this isn't some game," Efran Eason interrupted angrily.

"You could've fooled me," Fargo said.

"The judge came down here to help you help yourself," Eason insisted.

"He's got a heart of gold. You all do." Fargo smiled.

Judge Hibbs exchanged a quick glance with Efran Eason and returned his eyes to the big man on the other side of the bars. "You seem determined to meet under more formal conditions, Mr. Fargo," he said, his lips pursed.

Fargo shrugged. "It'll be her word against mine," he said.

The judge turned on his heel and strode from the building, a thin, lanky form followed by the mayor's short portly figure, Sheriff Sideman bringing up the rear, like two crows following a crane.

Fargo returned to the cot. Eason and the sheriff knew by now that he was onto what they were trying to do, but he wondered about Judge Hibbs. Had the judge simply been doing his friends a favor or did he have more of a part in it? Only one thing was unmistakably clear: Eason and the sheriff both wanted Frank Tupper back with a desperation that seemed more personal than just the pursuit of a thief and a killer. Yet perhaps they were both simply vengeful as well as zealous defenders of the town's interests. He wondered how much further they'd try to carry on with their charade before giving up on him. He stretched out and closed his eyes to wait.

He didn't get his answer until most of the morning had passed and he felt the stab of hunger in the pit of his stomach. The outside door flew open and Sheriff Sideman entered, drawing his six-gun as he opened the cell door. "March," he rasped. "In front of me. Judge Hibbs wants to see you." He steered Fargo down the street a hundred yards and turned him inside a building that bore a plaque.

Town Hall and Courthouse, Fargo read as he went into a room with five rows of wooden seats and a court bench at the front. Judge Warren Hibbs was the sole person in the room, seated behind the bench, his long face severe as he stared at Fargo. The sheriff walked his prisoner to the judge's bench and stepped back a few paces, and the judge fixed Fargo with a baleful stare.

"You're most lucky, Mr. Fargo." The judge frowned. "Mayor Eason has decided to drop all charges."

Fargo allowed a slow smile to move across his face. "Smart man, the mayor," he commented.

"Efran Eason is acting out of concern for his wife. He wants to spare her any embarrassment," Hibbs said sternly.

"Very touching," Fargo said, and the judge showed nothing in his long, thin face.

"Dismissed," Judge Hibbs said.

Fargo looked at the sheriff. "Come to my office and pick up your gun," Sheriff Sideman said almost genially, and strolled away.

Fargo watched him go with a frown. The mayor and he had lost, their little game failed, and the man's seeming unconcern didn't fit. He had expected bitterness, or at least chagrin. Fargo began to walk from the courtroom when a side door opened and the girl stepped into the room.

"You coming, Father?" she said to the judge, and halted as she saw Fargo. "I'm sorry. I thought you were alone," she apologized.

"I'm finished, Jennifer," the judge said, and Fargo took in the girl. She had dark-brown hair with a streak of lighter brown that ran down one side, a soft flowing curl to it as it hung to her shoulders. She was tall, with her father's loose figure but high, sharply pointed breasts pushed out the loose tan shirt she wore with a bold insouciance. A riding skirt cut fairly short revealed long, shapely calves. Her face held some of her father's length in it, but a straight nose, finely etched lips, and gray eyes under arching eyebrows gave her an aquiline loveliness. He saw her glance linger on his face, move across his powerful figure, a quick but thorough appraisal mirrored in the gray eyes. "Let's go, my dear," the judge said to the girl as he headed for the side door of the courtroom.

Fargo walked outside, paused, and watched the judge climb into a yellow-wheeled buckboard; the girl took the reins. Fargo caught her glance at him as she drove off and he watched the rig roll down the street. She sat with her back very straight and drove well, he saw. A very good-looking young woman, he decided and waited and watched until he saw the buckboard leave at the south end of town before he walked to the sheriff's office and got his Colt and gun belt back.

Sheriff Sideman continued to appear unbothered, almost casual, and Fargo stabbed at him to try to get under his surface calm. "My regards to the mayor and his wife," he said, and saw that the attempt had failed as the sheriff only nodded pleasantly.

"I'll do that," he said, and Fargo walked from the jailhouse and found the Ovaro hitched to the post. He took the horse by the reins and walked away feeling unexplainably uneasy. He still couldn't see the sheriff and the mayor as such good losers, not after all they'd tried.

The late-afternoon shadows began to stretch across the town and he stopped at the dance hall, surveyed the few men at the bar, and sat down at a table. He ordered a beef sandwich and the girl who brought it to him was not the same one who'd served him the bourbon. But the woman in the blue dress was at the bar and obviously the madam. He ate slowly, let the night fall, and finally made his way to Molly's cottage.

He felt the frown touch his brow as he dismounted. The door to the house hung open and he called out.

No one answered and his hand was on the butt of the Colt as he moved to the open doorway and peered inside. "Molly," he called again, but there was only silence, and when he stepped inside, he saw the two chairs upended on the floor, dishes from the table spilled onto the floor nearby. Alarm jabbed at him, and he saw the door to Amy's room open and he reached it in a half-dozen long strides. The room was empty but a wood dresser in one corner had three drawers pulled out and pieces of child's clothing hung from the bottom one. It was plain that the two had been hurriedly emptied out.

He whirled and felt the fury spiraling inside him. They'd taken both Molly and little Amy. Sheriff Sideman's unbothered casualness had been suddenly explained. "The bastards. The goddamn, stinking sons of bitches," Fargo murmured through lips that hardly moved. He strode from the house and slammed the door shut behind him, a cold rage churning inside him.

2

Fargo swung onto the Ovaro, the anger riding with him as he headed for the sheriff's office. He was unsurprised to find it locked and empty. He hailed a man driving a platform-spring grocery wagon and the man slowed. "You know where the mayor lives?" Fargo asked.

"Sure do. A mile north of town, gray house with a steep roof. You can't miss it," the man said.

Fargo waved back and took the Ovaro out of town at a fast trot. The house was easy enough to find, standing alone, two floors high, an example of misplaced Victorian architecture. Lights were on at the ground floor and he dismounted and strode to the door to pound three times insistently. A thin, small woman answered.

"The mayor in?" Fargo asked.

"He doesn't usually see people at home without an appointment," the woman said.

"He'll see me," Fargo said, and brushed past her to find himself inside a living room filled with fussy antimacassars and doilies on every piece of spindly furniture. Efran Eason's short form rose from a chair, Sheriff Sideman next to him. "Sort of figured I'd find you here," Fargo said to the sheriff, his voice cold steel. He took a step toward both men and the sheriff stiffened at once.

"Don't do anything you'll be sorry for, Fargo," the man warned.

"Where are they, you stinkin' bastards?" Fargo growled.

Efran Eason pulled indignation into his hesitant, round face. "We don't know," he said.

Fargo's blow was a long right, brought up in a looping arc that smashed with stunning force into Efran Eason's jaw. The man's feet left the ground as he hurtled backward to smash into a cupboard that shattered into pieces. He slid to the floor and lay still. Fargo turned to the sheriff, the Colt already in his hand.

"He was telling the truth," the sheriff said quickly as he backed away. "We don't know where she is."

"Bullshit. You set it up," Fargo growled.

"Maybe, but we don't know where she is," Sideman insisted. "That's the way it was set up."

"What does that mean?" Fargo frowned.

"We figured you'd come running for us, but we can't tell you what we don't know," the sheriff said. "They're safe someplace. That's all we know."

"Somebody knows, goddammit."

"Only the men who took them," the sheriff said.

"Then you get to them or this town's going to need a new sheriff and a new mayor," Fargo threatened.

"We can't. We don't know where they are, and killing us won't find them for you. That's why it was planned this way, so there's only one thing for you to do," the sheriff said. "You want the girl and her daughter to stay safe, you find Frank Tupper for us."

Fargo swore inwardly. There was a perverse cleverness to the way it had been set up, a cleverness beyond the reach of these two weasels, he was certain. But maybe all the doors weren't closed, yet.

The sheriff's voice broke into his racing thoughts. "Find Frank Tupper for us and the girl and her daughter will be released. That's the deal."

"Not yet, it isn't," Fargo snapped, and turned on his heel.

"Where are you going?" the sheriff said, surprise in his voice.

"To think about it," Fargo said from the doorway.

"There's nothing to think about, not now, not anymore," Sheriff Sideman protested.

"Stick close to your office," Fargo threw back. He heard Eason moaning as he strode from the house. He leapt onto the Ovaro and galloped back to town. Maybe they hadn't closed off all the doors yet. He reined to a halt in front of the dance hall, swung from the saddle, hurried into the building, and spotted the woman in the blue dress at her usual spot by the bar. She saw him enter, and professional that she was, she picked up the anger in his face as he strode toward her.

"Easy now, big man," she said soothingly. "Whatever it is, we can work it out."

"Which one of your girls wears the initial S on her bracelet?" Fargo asked gruffly.

The woman's lips pursed in thought. "That'd be big Susie," she said.

"That fits," Fargo said. "Where is she?"

"Jesus, she's suddenly awful popular," the madam said.

Fargo felt the stab of alarm at once. "Meaning what?" he frowned.

"Feller just came in and took her off for the evening," the woman answered. "Paid me twenty dollars, he did."

"Damn," Fargo bit out. "How long ago?"

"Ten minutes, maybe."

"You see which way he went with her?" Fargo pressed.

"Charlie, our sweeper, was outside. He told me had a horse waiting for her, put her on it, and rode north," the woman said.

Fargo spun and half-ran half-pushed his way through the crowded room. Once outside, he paused to scan the tracks in the ground outside. Too damn many, he swore silently, but leading the Ovaro behind him, he began to walk north, his eyes peering hard at the ground. With the special ability that was his, that extra something that made him what he was, he swept the tracks along the ground, his eyes moving from left to right and back again. Part training, part skill, part outer lore, part inner wisdom, he read the hoofprints the way other men read books, each print a letter taken alone, a sentence when put together. He sorted out the lone horseman's prints, the riders who rode in threes or more, and concentrated on those marks that indicated two horses traveling together.

There were entirely too many of those, he swore, but he continued to scan each set of prints until he found the subtle variation he sought and and his eyes narrowed. Two horses, traveling close together, but one constantly a little ahead of the other, as if leading the second horse along. The tracks continued north and suddenly veered from the road and up a fairly steep hillside. Now they were only two sets of prints to be seen and easy to follow as they turned sharply up a rise and into an area thickly grown with cottonwoods. Fargo moved after them and the rise grew higher, turning into a flat stretch that ended at the end of the ledge. He saw the two figures there, the woman naked, the burly man with his trousers off.

"That's it, baby, might as well enjoy it one last

time," the man said as, with a groan, he finished his pleasuring.

Fargo halted, slid from the saddle, and saw the woman half-rise up on her elbows as the man drew back into his haunches. "What's that mean, one last time?" she asked.

The man uttered a harsh laugh. "It means this is the end of the road for you, whore," he said.

Fargo drew his Colt as he raced forward. He wanted the girl alive. Maybe she could furnish a lead for him, something beyond Sideman or Eason. He saw the girl, suddenly aware of impending death, start to rise as the man, his trousers up and buckled, started toward her. She turned to run, stumbled, and before she could regain her footing, he had hold of her, his hands closing around her hair. She screamed in pain as he yanked her head back and her shapeless, flapping breasts bounced.

"Let her go," Fargo shouted, the Colt held in his outstretched hand. He saw the man spin in surprise. "Let go, *now*," Fargo said. But the man pulled on the woman, twisted, and swung her in front of him. He took a long step backward to halt at the very edge of the ledge.

"Drop the gun or she goes over," the man shouted. "It's a hundred feet down to the rocks." Fargo halted, keeping the Colt trained on the man. But the woman's ample figure hid him almost completely. "Drop the gun," the man snarled again.

"Let go of her," Fargo said, and held his position when he saw the man's right arm move back and down to his hip. Fargo dived to his left, hit the ground, and rolled as the man's gun fired, three shots from behind his shield. Fargo rolled again, into thicker brush as a fourth shot plowed into the ground a scant six inches from him. He grimaced as he held the Colt poised to fire, but the man still held his captive squarely in front of him. Fargo moved, a quick motion in the brush, and the man fired again, the shot off the mark yet close enough. Fargo swore, his eyes hardening as they swept the scene. The man continued to keep the woman in front of him, one arm around her neck, but his legs were planted wide apart, his right ankle clearly in view. It was just about the only part of him not covered by the woman's naked form. Fargo brought the Colt down, aimed, and fired.

"Jesus," the man screeched in pain as the bullet smashed through his ankle. He dropped to one knee, unable to stop himself, and Fargo saw the woman tear herself away in terror. As she started to spin away, the man grabbed at her, got his arm around her right leg, and pulled. Off balance, her overweight form went backward into him and Fargo heard his own curse as she started to go over the edge, arms flailing. "No . . ." the man screamed as she took him with her.

Fargo rose to his feet as they both disappeared over the edge of the ledge. Their screams mingled as they fell, but the dull, thudding sound that rose up from the bottom of the cliff was almost one.

Fargo ran to the edge and stared down and swore silently. If the woman had anything to help him, it was past history now. The man, too. They'd wanted her silenced, unable to talk about anything to anyone, and they'd sent someone to do the job. They'd gotten their way, though not exactly how they'd planned it.

He walked back to the Ovaro, reloaded the Colt, and rode down the side of the rise, a furrow digging into his brow. They'd been lucky just now. But they had also been very clever and very thorough. Too much so for the mayor and the sheriff, he mused again. He sent the horse back to town when he reached the road, and this time he halted a cow-hand who had just emerged from the dance hall. "You know where the judge lives? Judge Hibbs?" Fargo asked.

"Couple of miles west of town, along Oak Road. Go right at the first bend," the man said.

Fargo nodded, turned the horse, and rode west at a gallop. He found the line of oaks along one side of a road and turned at the bend. The house came into view a few minutes later, an oversize ranch house with a big bay window in front, a cherrywood door, and a landscaped garden to one side. The Trailsman halted the Ovaro in front of the heavy door, stepped back, and surveyed the house again. An L-shaped wing stretched back from the right side with a barn a dozen feet from the end. He stepped to the door, knocked, and waited, his wild-creature hearing picking up the sounds of footsteps inside. The door opened and the young woman faced him, a deep-red, floor-length silk robe adding to her tallness.

A tiny furrow touched her smooth brow. "You're the man from the courtroom," she said.

"You've a good memory," Fargo growled. "Where's the judge?"

"I enjoy memorizing people, places, things," she said, and regarded him for another moment. "Are you always so grim?"

"Depends," he said. "Now, where's the judge?"

"It's too late to come calling. See him in the courtroom tomorrow morning," the young woman said stiffly. She started to close the door. Fargo's hand shot out and sent it flying open and she stepped back, surprise in the gray eyes.

"Now, dammit," he snapped. The neck of the red silk robe fell open to reveal the line of one white mound.

"I'll handle this, Jennifer," the voice interrupted, and Fargo saw the judge stepping from an adjoining room, a Remington Army rifle in his hand.

Fargo eyed the gun and half-smiled. "You always come to the door this way, Judge?" he ventured.

"Sheriff Sideman was here. He told me you were very agitated and that you might show up," Judge Hibbs said. His long, thin face showed no expression, Fargo saw. The judge was a controlled man.

"What's this all about, Father?" Jennifer interrupted. "Who is this man and what does he want?"

"This man wants to know where Molly Mason is," Fargo snapped back, his eyes on the judge.

"I don't know anything about that," Judge Hibbs answered.

"Hell you don't. How deep are you in all this?"

"I want to see Frank Tupper returned, if that's what you mean. He's a very dangerous man. But the mayor and the sheriff have handled everything else. I don't always approve of the way they do things, but they have the best interests of the community at heart."

"That's a real nice speech, considering it's a crock of shit." Fargo saw the man's eyes harden. "I think you're up to your eyeballs in this."

"You've no reason to talk to my father that way," Jennifer Hibbs interrupted angrily, her dark eyes flashing.

Fargo's smile was wrapped in ice. "I'm paying him a compliment. He's the only one smart enough to plan this out," Fargo said.

"Get out, mister. I won't hear any more accusations or sarcasm from you. You've a problem, see Eason or Sideman," the judge said. "It's all in their hands."

"Sure it is," Fargo said. He cast a glance at Jennifer Hibbs as she watched him with a frown that held as much curiosity as protectiveness.

He backed out and away from the house, swung onto the Ovaro, and rode away. The visit had confirmed what he suspected in spite of the man's careful denials. Judge Hibbs had revealed more than he realized in explaining the rifle in his hands. The sheriff had stopped by to warn him. Fargo was sure Sideman didn't stop by to warn the judge about every angry gunslinger that showed up. But he'd made a fast trip this time because it was important the judge stay informed. Hibbs was the brains behind all of it, he was certain. He frowned all the way to town and finally came to a halt at Molly's house.

He tied the Ovaro in the back of the house and went inside, turned on a lamp, and examined both rooms inch by inch. But after he turned up nothing to help him, he undressed and stretched out on the bed where he'd lain with Molly. His jaw grew tight and the icy anger throbbed inside him. The bastards thought that they had him nailed down, that there was nothing he could do but what they wanted of him. They were at least partly right. He had to go along with them for Molly and Amy. But it wouldn't be quite the way they'd planned. Two could play with their rules, he grimaced, closed his eyes, his plans already firmly formed.

When morning came, he washed, dressed, and rode the Ovaro through the wakening town to halt at the jailhouse. Sheriff Sideman emerged and behind him, his jaw still swollen all out of shape, came Efran Eason. "You win, I guess," Fargo said. "I'll be going after him tomorrow. Meanwhile, I need to know more, everything I can." He smiled inwardly at the look of triumph the sheriff and the mayor exchanged.

"We'll be sending six men with you," the sheriff said.

"What the hell for?"

"You do the trailing, they'll do the capturing."

"I'll bring him back. You've Molly and the girl," Fargo protested. "I've got to bring him back."

"We want to be sure. Besides, you might need help. You never know what you'll meet along the way. They'll go along," Sideman said.

Fargo's thoughts raced. It was a complication but not one that would basically change anything, except at the start. "There's a long ridge lined with oaks due east of here. Bring them there at dawn," Fargo said. "Now, tell me about Frank Tupper."

"He doesn't look like the thieving killer he is," the sheriff said. "Sort-of soft-spoken, actually. He'll fool you."

"That's nothing I can follow," Fargo snapped.

"He's thin, medium build. But he rides a rocking-chair horse. That's something for you," the sheriff said.

"Likes a heavy horse with a short ride, huh?" Fargo said.

"He's got a big gray that's part standardbred and a little Percheron thrown in."

Fargo turned the sheriff's information in his mind. It would help, such as it was. "Anything else?" he barked.

"He was seen riding southeast, into the Uinta Mountains. That's heavy forest country," the sheriff said.

"Sure not the fastest way for running," Fargo said.

"Maybe hiding's more important than running to him," Sideman offered. Fargo half-shrugged, and as he turned his eyes on Efran Eason, he saw fear spring into the man's hesitant face instantly.

"Dawn on the ridge," Fargo said.

"No warnings about taking care of Molly Mason and the girl, Fargo?" Efran Eason sneered.

"Nope," Fargo said.

"Always glad to see a man who knows when he has no cards left," the mayor sneered again.

"Me, too," Fargo agreed. He turned the Ovaro and rode slowly away. Once out of town, he climbed a low hill and found a good shade tree with widespread limbs. He dismounted and stretched out on the grass and let thoughts idle through his mind as the hours ticked slowly away. The six men that were going to ride with him had been an unexpected development. They'd perhaps complicate things a little, especially at the start, but not enough to make him change his plans. There was nothing to do now but wait, and he let himself doze some until dusk began to filter down over the land. He rose, led the Ovaro to a patch of good bluegrass and a stream, and let the horse drink and eat his fill. When dark followed the dusk, he swung into the saddle and rode westward. By the time the moon appeared over the treetops he was a still, silent dark shape in the trees a dozen yards from the oversized ranchhouse.

Lights were on in parts of the house and he glimpsed Judge Hibbs through the bay window. When the light went on in a nearby room, he saw a table set for dining and a servant woman bringing in dishes. He saw Jennifer Hibbs sit down at the table, the judge taking a seat across from her. Candles on the dinner table gave her streak of light-brown hair a lustrous sheen.

Fargo watched and waited in silence as the night grew long. The servant woman dropped out of sight and he saw a light go on in the rear of the house. Jennifer Hibbs rose from the table and never returned.

Fargo leaned forward in the saddle, his eyes sweeping the house. They came to a halt on the light that went on in the center of the long low wing at the right, and he moved the Ovaro sideways through the trees until he had a better view of the window.

Jennifer Hibbs was inside the room and he glimpsed a four-poster bed with a canopy overhead. He watched the young woman remove her shoes and then her blouse. She wore a white slip under the garment that covered her modestly enough, but he saw smooth, square shoulders and high, round mounds that pulled the slip taut, Jennifer went to the window as he watched, and drew the curtain closed but he had seen all he'd come to see. His eyes scanned the side of the house where rhododendron bushes grew almost to the edge of the windowsill. His gaze traveled down to the end of the long house, held for a moment, and returned to the living room as the light went on. The judge was the last to retire and the house finally grew still, but Fargo continued to wait until the moon neared the midnight sky.

He moved the Ovaro to the very edge of the trees and slipped out of the saddle, silent as a mountain lion on a ledge. He moved across the ground in a half-crouch, passed the house, and went to the barn, where a small kerosene lamp burned on low yet gave enough light for him to see that the barn held four horses as well as the buckboard. He moved past the horses and chose a dark-gray filly with a good chest and strong legs. Lifting a saddle from the wall, he put it on the horse, and when he had the filly saddled and bridled, he led her out of the barn. He left the filly at the rear of the house and hurried forward to where the back door beckoned. But the door was locked.

Fargo drew the narrow, double-edged blade from its calf holster and began to work it into the opening beneath the lock. He worked carefully and silently, cutting into the soft wood of the doorjamb until he felt the lock give way. The door swung inward and he caught at the doorknob at once and guided it silently against the wall. He left it hanging open as he holstered the blade and started along the corridor to the center of the house. The doors to the first two rooms were open but the third was closed, and he put his face to the door and drew in a deep breath. The scent of powder and cologne touched his nostrils. He closed one big hand around the doorknob and turned it slowly, noiselessly.

He saw the big four-poster bed first, the silk canopy covering it, and he closed the door as silently as he'd opened it. He crossed the room on silent strides, the kerchief in his hand, and he halted at the side of the bed. Jennifer Hibbs looked small, almost doll-like, in the big bed; she wore a full-length, light-blue silk nightgown cut low enough at the neck to reveal the sweet curves of high, round breasts. He reached over to where she lay almost in the center of the bed, the kerchief held taut between both hands, paused for a second, and then brought it down over her mouth. Her eyes snapped open, but before she could gather herself, he had flipped her over, tied the kerchief behind her neck, and turned her back to him. Her eyes, wide with surprise and a hint of fear, stared at him over the kerchief as he took a half-step backward.

"Don't try to take off the kerchief," he growled. "Don't try to scream or make any kind of noise. I don't want to have to hurt you." Her brow drew a deep furrow across it and the gray eyes bored into him. "We're going on a little trip, you and I," Fargo said. "You can come along the hard way or the easy way, but you are coming along. You understand me?"

Jennifer nodded but he saw only fury in her eyes

now. She murmured something unintelligible behind the kerchief and he took another step backward.

"Get out of bed," he said, and she obeyed, sliding herself over the edge and revealing nicely rounded knees. "Get yourself some traveling clothes, enough to last a spell, and put them in a sack," Fargo ordered.

Her frown deepened as she stared at him. He motioned for her to move and she went to her closet as he stayed beside her. She picked out shirts, blouses, Levi's, and riding skirts and put them into a cloth sack. At one point, as she was bending over to pick up a shirt, he saw her pause, her hand start to slide up toward the kerchief. "Don't try it, honey," Fargo growled. "Or I'll have to finish and you mightn't like what I pick to take along."

Her hand dropped and she continued gathering clothes as he watched. She had a long, sinuous figure with a flat, narrow rear that hardly bulged the nightgown. When she finished stuffing the sack, she drew a light cape over herself and took a moment to glare at him. He took her elbow and walked her across the room and into the corridor, then to the rear door.

Outside, he saw her eyes widen even further when she saw the gray filly waiting there. "That's your horse, isn't it?" Fargo said. "I figured as much. She fits you." He gestured and she climbed up, the nightgown riding up to show one very lovely, long thigh. He took the filly by the bridle and led the way to where he'd left the Ovaro. When he swung upon the pinto, he rode away with the reins of her horse in his hand, a slow walk first, then going into a trot and finally into a fast canter.

They rode west. The moon was starting to slide down the sky when they reached the oaks that lined the ridge. They rode into the deep darkness of the trees and Fargo dismounted.

Jennifer dropped to the ground and he didn't stop her this time as she yanked the kerchief from her mouth. "You are going to be hung when my father catches up to you," she spit out, her gray eyes flashing.

"That's been tried before," Fargo said laconically.

"Just what do you think you're doing?" she threw at him. "What's the meaning of all this?"

"I'll talk about it tomorrow. Right now I want to get some shut-eye," he said. He took a length of lariat, wrapped it around her wrists, and tied the other end to his own wrist. He allowed six feet of rope between them, and when he finished, he lowered himself against the base of a thick oak. She still glared at him.

"It's a warm night," he told her. "You'll be fine as you are. Now you can stand there all night or you can go lie down someplace. Makes no matter to me, honey. But you'll be riding most of tomorrow, I promise you that."

He closed his eyes and heard her finally move to settle herself on the ground, the rope around her wrist stretched almost taut. He opened his eyes enough to peer at her and saw she'd put the cape over herself, more for modesty than warmth. She felt confident about the judge rescuing her, come morning, and decided to just wait, he realized.

He snapped awake only twice during the night as the rope on his wrist tugged, but each time it was because she'd turned restlessly in her sleep. When dawn hung at the edge of the day, the disciplined clock inside him went off and he sat up and undid the rope around his wrist.

The motion woke Jennifer and she pushed up onto her elbows, blinked sleep away, and frowned across the small space between them. "It's still dark," she muttered.

"For another ten minutes or so," he said. "Get up and get dressed." He walked to her, helped pull her to her feet, and undid the lariat around her wrists. She bent down, holding the cape around her, and pulled things from the sack.

"I'm not going to dress with you looking on," she snapped.

"Correction, honey. From now on you're going to do whatever I tell you to do," Fargo said mildly. "But I'm feeling kindly this morning, so I'll turn my back."

"How gallant," she snapped, icy sarcasm coating each word. He listened to her as she pulled the nightgown off and drew on clothes. He turned when she was just buttoning the shirt and caught a glimpse of the edge of one high, round breast. She'd put on a dark-blue shirt and a black riding skirt. He held the reins of her horse and ordered her up.

"Where are we going now?" she asked as he swung onto the Ovaro.

"To find a nice spot for you to wait."

"Wait for what?"

"For me to get back to you."

"I demand to know why you're doing this," she said stiffly. "You promised you'd explain today."

"The day's young yet, Jenny." Fargo smiled.

"Jennifer," she corrected tartly.

"Whatever," he said as he drew to a halt. He'd gone near a half-mile, plenty far enough even if she somehow worked the gag free. "Hit the ground," he muttered, and Jennifer Hibbs slid from the dark-gray filly. He had the lariat around her instantly, pulled her against a medium-trunked oak, and tied her to the tree with quick loops of the rope.

"Wait! What are you doing?" she protested.

"Making sure you'll be here when I come back for you," Fargo said.

"You can't leave me here like this," she protested, anger and alarm in her gray eyes. She tried to wriggle free but quickly realized she was bound tight. "What if an Indian comes along, a Ute or an Arapaho?"

"Be polite," Fargo answered as he put the kerchief around her mouth and tied it securely. "I won't be long. Enjoy the sunrise." He rode away as she screamed muffled protests after him behind the kerchief. It would be an unlikely chance that any Utes would come upon her, he knew, and if they did, they'd spend hours being careful and wondering why she was tied to the tree. He'd be back long before then.

He rode slowly back along the edge of the trees. He was in no hurry. They'd wait, he was certain, and when he reached the beginning of the ridge where the line of oaks began, he moved into the open and saw the horsemen waiting below. Mayor Eason and Sheriff Sideman sat their horses together, the other six men across from them. Fargo expected a seventh visitor and his glance swept the terrain in the background as he rode to a halt.

"These are the men that will ride with you, Fargo," Sideman said. "Abe Tollman, on the bay, heads them up."

Fargo's eyes went to the man and saw a hooked nose on a heavy face, black hair sticking out from under a faded tan stetson. He took in the man's outfit, let his glance move over the others. They were all hired guns, all men with jaded eyes and faded hopes, the kind of men who lived by taking the jobs few others wanted. He let each one's eyes meet his for a moment and then turned away. None had that quality he looked for in a man's eyes, that spark that meant he could be more than mere trouble. His eyes went to Eason and the sheriff.

"They follow my orders or else," Fargo said.

"They understand. They're going along to help you," Sideman said unctuously.

Fargo grunted deliberately at his words. "If you say so," he murmured. He paused, sought for something to prolong the moment. "One thing you ought to know. Anything happens to Molly Mason and her daughter, and I'll come after you."

"You bring back Frank Tupper and they'll be safe and sound and in your hands, Fargo," the sheriff said.

Fargo's eyes went past the man, across the open land where the racing horseman appeared. He started to turn the Ovaro away, but the man's shout reached him and he saw Eason and Sideman turn in surprise.

"Stop him. Stop that bastard," the shout came. Fargo halted as Judge Hibbs galloped up. "Where's Jennifer? Where's my daughter?" the judge yelled.

"What are you talking about, Warren?" Eason frowned.

"Jennifer, he took Jennifer," Judge Hibbs accused. The judge moved toward Fargo, his long face contorted with fury. "You took her, damn you," he snarled. "Where is she?"

"Where's Molly Mason and Amy?" Fargo returned. He watched the man pull his face into some form of composure as he shot a glance at Eason and Sideman.

"I wouldn't know. Where's Jennifer?" Hibbs answered.

"I wouldn't know," Fargo said.

"You're lying!"

"That makes two of us," Fargo said calmly, and then, his voice turning into cold steel, he leaned forward in the saddle and his eyes were blue agates as they bored into Warren Hibbs. "You started this, all of you, but two can play this game. Molly will be safe if I bring back Frank Tupper. I have your word on it. Only your word's as good as a straw house in a twister. I bring him back and maybe you'll decide Molly and Amy are loose ends you can't afford to leave around. Well, it's different now."

Warren Hibbs stared back but swallowed hard. "You can't do this. You can't hurt Jennifer," he muttered.

"Then you'd damn well better keep Molly and the girl safe and alive," Fargo rasped.

"Jennifer had nothing to do with any of this," the judge protested.

"Neither did Molly. That didn't bother you. It doesn't bother me now," Fargo said coldly.

Hibbs looked at the mayor and the sheriff, uncertainty in his eyes.

"He goes after Frank Tupper," Eason said with surprising firmness. "We'll keep the girl safe. It'll all work out just fine, Warren."

Fargo's face was as if carved in granite. "It better." He pulled the pinto into a half-circle and rode off. The six gunhands fell in behind him and rode a dozen yards back. Olson hadn't been anywhere in sight and it was plain he was with Molly and Amy somewhere.

Fargo rode up along the ridge, glanced down, and saw the judge riding away with Eason and Sideman. They vanished from sight in the distant trees and Fargo moved forward, the grimness staying inside him. He'd dealt himself one ace-in-a-hole, but there are a hundred ways the game could go sour. He'd no choice now but to play it out to the end.

3

Jennifer Hibbs' eyes were a gray glare as he undid the kerchief.

"Daddy sends regards," Fargo murmured.

"Bastard," she hissed.

He smiled back. "No flattery, please," he said, and loosened the ropes that tied her to the tree and, in one deft motion, had a loose bond around her wrists. "That's so you can ride but not get any ideas," he said, and turned to the six men who had halted when he reached Jennifer. His eyes swept the six and he waited when one of them spoke up, a wiry-built man with a down-turned mouth.

"You goin' to take her all the way with us?" the man asked.

"All the way," Fargo said. "She'll be my problem, my responsibility. That means you leave her alone. It also means I'll kill anyone that even thinks of helping her escape."

"Big talk, Fargo," the man said with a sneer.

"Who are you, cousin?" Fargo asked.

"Biddle. Joe Biddle," the man said.

"Well, Biddle, it's more than talk. I don't want any of you along in the first place, so I'll be happy to get rid of any or all of you. Don't push me," Fargo said.

He saw the man glance at the others and try to mask uneasiness with hollow bravura. Biddle would be trouble, Fargo knew, a small man who had to put on big airs. He waited as Biddle brought his eyes back to him.

"I'm not ready, big man," Biddle said.

"Whenever." Fargo brought the dark-gray filly to Jennifer.

She mounted the horse with no difficulty, her wrist ropes giving her enough play to hold the reins without discomfort. She swung her horse beside him as he moved forward, the six gunhands staying a dozen yards back. He took the one road east after he left the ridge, the one that bordered the forest that rose into the Uinta Mountains, confident it was the path Frank Tupper would logically have taken when he first fled. Jennifer's voice cut into his thoughts, fire and ice in her tone.

"Explain. You said you would. Why am I here?" she snapped.

"Might as well start properly. The name's Fargo . . . Skye Fargo," he began.

"It's a little late for proper behavior. Besides, I know who you are. I asked Father about you after your visit last night," she said.

"What'd he tell you?" Fargo asked. "This ought to be interesting."

"You're the man who refused to trail Frank Tupper for the sheriff and Mayor Eason," she said.

"That all he said?" Fargo questioned.

"No. He said you were imagining things about the sheriff and Mayor Eason," Jennifer added.

"Imagining, my ass," Fargo bit out. "I'll tell you the truth of it," he said, and proceeded to detail what had happened to Molly and Amy. "They took them and they're holding them to make me do what they want. If I want to keep Molly and the girl alive, I'll cooperate. They've been right clever about it, too," he finished bitterly.

"By *they* you mean Efran Eason and the sheriff," Jennifer said.

"I mean Eason, the sheriff, and your daddy. He's part of it," Fargo snapped.

"No, never. Daddy wouldn't be part of anything like that," Jennifer protested.

"He's in it up to his eyeballs," Fargo said coldly. "Only now he knows you are, too. They've got Molly and Amy. I've got you."

Jennifer cast a long, thoughtful glance at him. "How far?" she asked.

"How far what?" she frowned.

"How far will you go?" she went on.

He turned the question in his mind, realized all that it meant, and he was unwilling to face that final answer yet. "As far as I have to go, and that'll be up to them," he said.

She allowed a cynical smile. "You condemn them for what they did, but you go ahead and do the same thing. That makes you no better than they," she said.

"There's a difference," he said grimly.

"Where?"

"I'd no choice. They did," he said.

She took in the reply and fell silent.

He increased the Ovaro's pace as he turned with the road and saw it grow closer to the forest, which stretched up into the mountains. She kept pace with him, he saw, the dark-gray filly moving well, and by midday he halted at a stream to let the horses drink and rest.

The six gunhands kept pretty much to themselves and stayed back again as Fargo moved on, Jennifer beside him. She rode well, he noted, her long thighs firm against the horse, her back straight, and the round, high breasts hardly bounced.

As the road curved in toward the Uinta Moun-

48

tains, Fargo's gaze stared mostly down on the terrain, searching, probing, peering hard at every hoofprint that appeared. It was nearing dusk when he suddenly pulled up, swung from the saddle, and crouched down on the narrowing road. He ran his fingers along a series of hoofprints and carefully circled the edges of each print. "We've picked up his trail," he said as he rose. "A heavy horse, the prints deeper and broader than any of the others."

"Why didn't you pick them up before this?" Jennifer asked with an edge of tartness.

"They were mixed in with other prints. When the others turned off, they've come to show up clearly. He took the road into the mountains," Fargo said, and returned to the saddle. "It's nice to have a skeptic along to check up on me," he commented.

She allowed a wry half-smile. "I like to feel I'm being of some use."

"You are," he answered, and drew a quick glare.

"Not that way," she snapped. "And you're still wrong about my father being involved in whatever Mayor Eason and the sheriff may have done."

He saw the instant angry defensiveness in her eyes. Blood ties, loyalty, and love were not things easily shaken, he commented inwardly. "Then I'll have to apologize to him when the time comes," he said, unwilling to press deeper for the moment.

"Indeed," she snapped, her chin held high.

He peered through the gathering dusk and saw the road closing off to an end, swallowed up by thick brush and heavy tree cover behind. He called a halt.

"You men have rations with you?" he asked as the six hired guns rode up.

"We do," Abe Tollman said. "Depending on how long we're on the trail."

"We'll shoot some fresh game tomorrow," Fargo

said. He pulled the Ovaro to one side and took the dark-gray filly with him. "You'll share with me," he said to Jennifer as he sat down against the gray-brown bark of a box elder. She settled beside him as he took a long strip of beef jerky from his saddle-bag and gave her half.

"You intend keeping me tied all the time?" she asked between mouthfuls.

"Depends," he said.

"It's hard to get a straight answer out of you, isn't it?" she observed testily.

"Depends," he said, and drew a hiss of exasperation. The night stayed warm, and with nothing to cook there was no need for a fire. When he finished eating, he rose and looked down at her in the light of the new moon. "I'm going to turn in," he said, and took a blanket from the Ovaro and laid it on the ground. "You're welcome to share it," he said.

"No, thank you," Jennifer said stiffly.

He began to pull off clothes and he saw her watch his powerfully muscled body take shape before her eyes. She continued to watch him until, almost naked, he looked down at her.

"You going to sleep in your clothes?" he asked, and she pulled her eyes from his body to meet his gaze.

"I'm not going to change out here," Jennifer snapped. "And I can't with these ropes on."

He undid the ropes that loosely bound her wrists and she rose, started to take the sack of clothes into the trees when he reached out and his hand closed around her wrist. "Take what you need and leave the rest," he said softly.

"Suspicious?"

"Careful," he corrected.

She rummaged through the clothes and took out the nightgown and the cape and left the sack on the ground. He watched her go into the darkness of the trees, listened to her change, and when she returned, she held the cape in front of her. Once again he tied the ropes at her wrists to his, allowing at least six feet of length.

"You going to do that every night?" she asked, and snapped out an answer before he got his mouth open. "I know, *depends*."

"You're learning." He smiled. "I like that."

She lay down at the end of the rope and used the cape again to cover herself. Fargo closed his eyes and let sleep come quickly. He wasn't awakened until morning came and the rope around his wrist tugged. He lay still and opened his eyes to see the figure crouched beside Jennifer, who was up on her elbows. The man moved as he spoke in hushed tones to the girl and Fargo glimpsed the downturned mouth in the mean face. Joe Biddle, he murmured silently and watched through slitted eyes as the man finished and crawled away, rose to a crouch, and hurried back to the others, who, Fargo took note, were still sleeping. Jennifer lay back down and Fargo stayed motionless, feigning sleep until he saw Jennifer sit up and purposely let the lariat tug on his wrist.

He sat up, peered at her, and watched as she stood, kept the cape carefully around herself. "I'd like to wash and dress," she said. "I heard a stream back in the woods."

"Go ahead," he said, and undid the wrist bonds. He watched as this time she made no attempt to take the sack but picked out a blouse and Levi's and hurried into the dense woods. He had heard the stream himself, and he rose, pulled on his trousers, and watched the six men gather themselves. He listened to Jennifer in the woods and she finally returned, face shining and freshly scrubbed. He led

51

the way to where he had spotted a patch of blue-
berry, which served as breakfast. As he adjusted
the cinch straps on the Ovaro, his eyes flicked across
the others and he saw Biddle and Jennifer exchange
glances. He felt the hardness curl inside him, but he
finished with the cinch, mounted the horse, and
beckoned Jennifer to him. He bound her wrists
loosely to the saddle and drew an impatient hiss.

"I want to concentrate on trailing, not watching
you," he said, turned from her, and slowly walked
the Ovaro forward. His eyes swept the forest terrain. He finally picked up three prints, paused, and
went forward to his left.

Jennifer stayed close to him and he was aware
that she watched everything he did with concentra-
tion while the others stayed back, following single-
file. He moved forward at a slow walk, pausing
every few minutes, his lips pulled back in a grimace
as he scanned every piece of the thick forest. Not
only were the prints old but the heavy forest had a
carpet of thick moss, leaves, and switchgrass that,
heavy with its own moisture, sprang quickly back to
shape. Altogether, they let only an occasional print
show. He paused at each one before moving on to
the next, but he continued to find that next one
with an inexorable sureness. The noon hour had
slowly passed and he'd found another two prints
when Jennifer spoke up, a hint of awe in her voice.

"How do you know which way to go? It can't be
the prints alone," she said.

"It isn't," Fargo said. "Prints are only one part of
trailing. There are other things you have to look for
when it's tough going."

"Such as?"

"In a forest this thick, any animal as large as a
horse will leave other signs, low branches bent,
leaves that stay bruised, young twigs snapped."

"Any rider passing this way since could've snapped off twigs," she countered.

"Yes, but they'd have broken ends that are fresh and white. The twigs I'm looking at have discolored and turned yellow. They were snapped off at least a week back. Besides, this is no roadway. Other riders wouldn't likely be coming through here," Fargo answered. He halted, pointed to another pair of hoofprints that appeared in a soft place in the soil. "He came this way. Same heavy horse, the prints deep and spread out," Fargo murmured in satisfaction. Once again, he moved forward in the painstakingly slow, careful manner, and little by little more of the hoofprints came into sight.

The day began to move toward dusk when the thick forest suddenly erupted in a flurry of black-tailed jackrabbits. Fargo motioned to Abe Tollner. The man nodded and sent two of his men after the game, their shots echoing in the thick woods moments later. They returned with four of the big, rangy animals.

Fargo called a halt and pointed to a flattened spot amid the trees.

"He camped here. We'll do the same," he said.

The men quickly made a small fire, set up makeshift spits, and skinned and roasted the rabbits. Night fell and Fargo unsaddled the horses and undid Jennifer's wrist ropes so she could eat more comfortably, and she settled down beside him with a piece of the tender rabbit. He saw her eyes study him with cool respect.

"I can see why Eason and the sheriff needed you. Most trackers would have lost him long ago. You're very good," she said.

"Better than you know."

"A touch of conceit, I see."

"A touch of truth," he said, and saw the gray eyes studying him.

"Are you trying to tell me something?" she questioned.

"Maybe," he muttered.

"Say it right out," she snapped.

"Sometimes it's best to let things take their course. You learn more that way," Fargo said, and she continued to frown at him. "But I'll say this much. You don't turn off what's a part of you. A man makes a living being alert, probing, watching, especially for the little things. That stays. It never stops," he said.

Her gray eyes narrowed on him and he could see uncertain thoughts racing through her mind, but she kept those thoughts to herself and finished eating in silence.

While the fire burned down and the others prepared to sleep, Fargo took his bedroll from the pinto and laid it out.

"May I go into the trees and change?" Jennifer asked with a layer of iciness.

He nodded, but he noted that she only took the nightgown and cape from the sack, and he smiled inwardly.

When she returned, the cape on her shoulders, the fire still burned. She sat down near it, curled her legs under her, but one long, lovely calf remained visible. He started to look away when his eyes snapped back at the slender, sinuous shape that slid toward her, attracted by the warmth of the fire. He saw the light-brown base with the dark-brown markings of the prairie rattler, a snake he'd always considered misnamed, for it ranged far and wide beyond the prairie. The rattler edged closer to Jennifer's leg. She wasn't aware of it yet a scream and sharp motion would sure as hell send the snake's highly poisonous fangs into her. He had to prevent that reaction first.

"Listen to me, Jenny," he said, his voice low and calm. "Don't move and listen to me. Don't turn, don't look at anything. Just stay where you are." He saw her stiffen, alarm flood her face, but she stayed motionless as the rattler slid closer. He couldn't shoot, not from where he sat. The bullet that blasted the rattler would also smash into her. But the others had heard him and now peered across the embers, the snake equally visible to them. Fargo kept his voice low as he called across to them. "You've got a better angle. Shoot," he said.

Abe Tollner answered first. "I'm not that good a shot. I miss and it nails her. I'm not takin' on blame for that," he said.

Fargo's eyes flicked to the others, who stayed motionless.

"You brought her. It's your show, Fargo," Joe Biddle said.

Bastards, Fargo muttered inwardly. He pressed both palms on the soil, pushed himself slowly upward till he reached a crouch. The rattler continued to slide closer to Jennifer and she saw the snake now, her eyes wide and tiny beads of perspiration suddenly coating her smooth brow.

"Don't move," he said again, his voice low. He took a step forward, then another, his eyes on the snake as it slowed near the bottom of her foot. He saw its forked tongue flick out, probing, sensing flesh and warmth. A big reptile, it would deliver a lethal dose of venom, he knew. It could possibly pass Jennifer, but a glance at her face told him she'd not be able to remain motionless for more than a few dozen seconds more. He moved forward, a longer step, every muscle in his body tensed as he reached his right hand out. He'd only have one chance, he realized, one chance for Jennifer and for himself, for the rattler would strike, whirl, and strike again.

He ventured another soft step, his hand only inches away from the snake now, and he saw the strain in Jennifer's face at the breaking point. But he also saw the rattler come to a stop, suddenly aware of something different that had entered its circle of sensitivity. The rattler started to draw back to go into its striking coil, and Fargo's hand shot out, his fingers closing around the serpent just back of its head. The rattler's strong, sinuous body thrashed out instantly and Fargo heard Jennifer's scream as she flung herself backward. He could feel the snake's muscles throbbing beneath his grip and the serpent's furious rattling was so rapid and loud it sounded like steam escaping a valve. Turning, he flung the snake away from him and yanked the Colt from its holster as the rattler hit the ground. It started to streak for the brush, and Fargo fired, two shots, and the snake's head disappeared in a shower of blood and bone. The body still thrashed on the ground, the automatic reactions of nerves and muscles, until it finally grew still.

Fargo turned to Jennifer where she lay, face-down, trembling, and drew her to her feet. She clung to him for a moment, the cape still around her. He felt the soft, high firmness of her breasts against his chest.

When she drew away she looked up at him, composure coming back into her face. "Thank you," she murmured. "It could've bitten you, too."

"It could've," Fargo agreed.

"You risked your life for me," Jennifer said.

"I took a chance. Leave it at that," he said. She studied him a moment longer before turning away. His eyes went to the men across from him and they

56

turned away and began to settle down. He took the length of lariat and bound Jennifer's wrists again, leaving a longer length before attaching the end to his own wrist.

"I thought you might stop this," Jennifer said.

"You thought wrong," he grunted, and settled down on his bedroll. "Turn in. It'll be another long day tomorrow," he told her, and stretched out after stripping down to his underdrawers. He positioned the holster with the big Colt inside it against his right hand and seemed to close his eyes.

Jennifer moved as far away as the length of rope let her and settled down under the cape, and Fargo gave himself an hour to nap. When he woke, his eyes were mere slits but they let him see across the darkness to where Jennifer lay. He stayed awake, watched, and a little more than an hour passed when he saw the figure move toward her in a crouch.

He didn't need to see the man's face clearly. He knew very well who it was, and he watched as Biddle knelt on one knee beside Jennifer. Fargo saw her head come up and noticed that she was careful not to move her arm so the rope didn't tug at his wrist. He saw her shake her head, and straining his ears to the limit, he picked up Biddle's hoarse whisper.

"Come on, goddammit. You wanted out, you said," Biddle whispered. "This is what we talked about."

"Not now. Something's wrong. I'm afraid. Maybe another time," Fargo heard Jennifer say.

"This is the time. You want out and your daddy'll pay me high and handsome for bringing you back. Now shut up and come along," Biddle said, and Fargo saw the man take hold of Jennifer's wrist bonds, holding her still while he began to cut the rope with a knife.

"He knows, I tell you. Somehow, he knows," Jennifer said. "Let's wait a little longer. I don't want anybody hurt because of me."

"I'll take care of myself. You get your ass up," Biddle said, severing the ropes and returning the knife to his pocket. He started to get to his feet when Fargo slid the big Colt from its holster and sat up.

"You're a damn fool, Biddle," he said quietly, but his words carried through the stillness with icy clarity.

The man's head jerked up in surprise and Jennifer half-turned to stare across at Fargo as she froze in place.

"Son of a bitch," Biddle swore. He yanked at the gun at his side. It didn't clear the holster before Fargo's shot slammed into his chest. Biddle flew backward as though kicked by a mule, a small spray of red erupting from his chest. He was dead when he landed on his back and he lay still.

"Oh, my God," Fargo heard Jennifer gasp and turn away from the man's inert form.

The others, snapping awake, leapt to their feet, some with guns drawn. They stared at Joe Biddle as Fargo slowly walked toward the man.

"Bury him. Put him under a rock. Do whatever you want with him," Fargo said coldly. He turned away as the others began to drag the man's body across the ground, and Jennifer, standing, met his agate-blue eyes. "Over here," he growled, and she followed him to the bedroll; he bound her wrists again.

"That's what you were telling me, wasn't it?" she said. "You were waiting, ready."

"You tried to turn him away. I'll give you credit for that," Fargo said. "He was just stupid."

"Did you have to kill him?" she asked.

58

"He was going for his gun. Besides, he'd have tried again sometime," Fargo said.

Jennifer's gray eyes studied him once more, a furrow across her brow. "I think I understand something else you said, when I spoke about how you'd risked your life for me." She frowned. "I understand your answer now. It really wasn't for me. It was for Molly Mason, because you need me alive for the game you're playing."

"Don't look a gift horse in the mouth," Fargo said blandly.

"Perhaps not, but now that I've things clear, I don't need to make the mistake of being grateful," she said tartly.

"Not unless you want to be." He smiled. She spun away and settled herself on the ground, as distant as the shortened tether would allow. He lay down on the bedroll, his muscled body rippling and felt her eyes on him.

"At least you told me. You were honest enough. I just didn't understand," she said, and he heard the edge of bitterness in her voice.

"Go to sleep," he muttered, closed his eyes, and listened to her position the cape over herself before she fell silent. He'd disappointed her. She had liked the thought of someone risking his life for her. It was plainly something no one had ever done before. Had she wanted to be grateful? he wondered. There was a lot of steam under that cool, contained surface. Maybe he could give her another chance before the hunt was over, he mused.

The sun had to fight its way through the thickness of the forest foliage in the morning. Fargo let Jennifer use his canteen to wash. She put on another outfit, a yellow blouse and a black riding skirt, and managed to resemble a jonquil against the forest green. Her gray eyes were cool as she met his glance, and he motioned to Abe Tollner and the others to follow. She swung in alongside him and he rode on through the thick forest. The footprints of Frank Tupper's horse became more prominent as the earth grew softer and Fargo dismounted twice during the morning to press the forest floor with his hands.

"What's bothering you?" Jennifer asked after the second halt.

"This ground's awful moist," Fargo said.

"An underground spring somewhere near," he said.

"Been going on too long for that," he said. "But there's water somewhere." He moved forward, followed the prints, and glanced back to see Abe Tollner and the others riding single-file behind.

As he moved deeper into the forest, the character of the trees changed, suddenly becoming twisted and gnarled, branches reaching out toward the intruders like so many misshapen arms. Direct sun infiltrated the thick foliage only in sudden shards of yellow light and an occasional bright patch on the ground. The forest had suddenly become an uneasy place, dark and dank and made of twisted shapes. The air became heavy and he saw more and more patches of elf-cap moss on the rocks and decayed logs and large growths of liverworts on the base of the tree trunks. But the hoofprints continued on and Fargo followed and the day slid into the afternoon when he reined in and drew in a deep breath.

"You smell it?" he asked Jennifer.

"All I smell is damp earth and old wood," she said.

"You want to trail, you learn to use your nose just as you do your eyes and ears," Fargo said. "I smell smoke, cooking smoke."

"Indian camp?" she asked, and he shook his head. "How do know it isn't?" she pressed.

He drew in another deep breath and his nostrils flared. "White man's cooking. Roast venison. The Indians boil their meat mostly, and when they roast they roast small pieces heavy with bear grease. Besides, Indian cooking always smells of pemmican."

"A trapper's camp?" Jennifer ventured.

He shook his head again. "Too much, too strong," Fargo said. "Strange, but we keep following prints," he said, and moved forward.

The odor of cooking fires grew stronger as they advanced and clearly came from their left, beyond the thick forest growth, and Fargo saw the hoofprints he followed suddenly turn left along a narrow path that opened through the trees.

"Looks as though Frank Tupper followed his nose, too," Jennifer observed.

"Guess we'll be finding out," Fargo said, continuing to move slowly forward. The narrow path widened and the heavy tree growth suddenly thinned a little and the last light of the afternoon filtered down. He glanced back at Abe Tollner and the four men with him. They had closed ground and rode only a few paces back. Fargo returned his eyes to the moist earth and picked up another set of hoofprints. "We've got company," he muttered to Jennifer, and she glanced around quickly, alarm in her face.

"I don't see anybody," she said.

"I don't either. I feel them," he replied.

"They could be Utes. You could be wrong," Jennifer said.

"I could be, but I don't think so," Fargo said. He felt the question revolve inside him. If not Indians, if not trappers, then, who? The frown crept across his forehead, stayed as he moved forward, and he had gone perhaps another hundred yards when the figures rose up from the trees on both sides of the pathway.

Fargo, his hand resting on the butt of the Colt in its holster, reined to a halt as he scanned the forms that had appeared like so many wraiths materializing out of the twilight grayness. He saw both men and women—as many women as men, he noted—and he guessed there were some twenty-five in all. The men for the most part were bearded and wore shirts, suspenders, and trousers. The women, a mixture of ages, wore loose, somewhat formless dresses or tight-fitting buckskin outfits.

One of the men stepped forward, tall, with a black beard and black, burning eyes, a sternly righteous face that bore the mark of authority in it. "Who be you, travelers?" the man said in a booming voice.

"Searchers," Fargo answered, and saw that half the figures carried rifles close to their sides, both men and women. "Who be you?" he returned.

"We are the Promised Ones," the man said. "Our home is here in the forest, for now. I am Josiah."

"I'm Fargo, Skye Fargo. We're just passing through," the Trailsman said, and swept a glance over the others again. There were more women than men, he decided.

"No one just passes through. Everyone leaves a mark," Josiah intoned.

"I'll go with that," Fargo agreed.

"And everyone deserves a chance to be saved," the man said.

"If you say so," Fargo said carefully. He saw that the others hadn't moved as they looked on.

"I do say that. Come and break bread with us," Josiah said. "We have ample to share."

Fargo considered for a moment. "We'd be obliged,"

he said, and the man motioned for him to follow as he turned and the others began to close in behind him.

"Why are you doing this?" Jennifer whispered, irritation in her voice.

"Frank Tupper came this way. Maybe they can give us a lead. Besides, we can use a meal and a place to bed down."

"I don't like this," she muttered.

"Woman's intuition?"

"Yes," she snapped, and he said nothing. He'd seen it work far too often to scoff at it.

"Relax," he told her.

She tossed him a glare and stayed tense as the land suddenly came open and he saw the large cleared section, a semicircle of cabins and shacks at the perimeter. Two large fires took up the center of the cleared area, both burning under long spits that held meat being cooked.

Other figures emerged from the cabins as they arrived, and again he saw more women than men as well as at least fifteen children. One of the men motioned to him and he brought his horse to a rope tether as Jennifer followed. He dismounted as Josiah and two men came up.

"This is Abargus and Bartholomew," Josiah introduced. "They are my right-hand helpers. I leave your men to introduce themselves to my people."

"They will. This is Jennifer Hibbs," Fargo said.

"You are wed?" Josiah asked.

"No, just traveling companions," Jennifer put in quickly.

Josiah's smile had a definite note of satisfaction in it, Fargo frowned inwardly. The rest of Josiah's people had returned to their chores when the girl suddenly appeared almost as if by magic.

"Asa, come and welcome these good people,"

Josiah said, and she stepped forward, her eyes on Fargo.

A smallish girl, she wore a buckskin shirt that left her midriff bare, and a short, buckskin skirt that revealed lithe, firm young legs. Long black hair, a little unkempt, surrounded an olive-skinned face of even features, flashing black eyes, and warm, full lips.

"Hello, Asa," he said, and the girl came to him, extended her hand in a warm, firm grip. Her movements were quick, catlike, he decided as she half-turned to Jennifer. "This is Jennifer," Fargo introduced, and Asa swept a dismissing glance over her, still holding on to Fargo's hand. Finally she drew her hand back and shot Josiah a glance as he moved closer.

"Asa will get you anything you need," the man said.

"Don't figure to be needing much," Fargo said, and as his eyes swept the encampment again, he noted the small cross carved into the door of each cabin. "You Joseph Smith's followers?" he said.

"We are indeed followers of Joseph Smith," Josiah said. "Members of his church, the Church of the Latter-day Saints of Jesus Christ. But we are not followers of this Brigham Young. That is why we are here. We left those others who blaspheme the teachings of Joseph Smith."

"Why do you call yourselves the Promised Ones?" Jennifer asked, and Fargo caught the slight edge in her voice.

"Because we have been promised salvation and it shall be ours," the man said, his voice taking on righteousness. "We shall embrace all who join in the right with us and smite those who act against us."

"Such as Brigham Young's followers?" Jennifer queried.

"Exactly. They care only for power. They have lost the key to the spirit," Josiah said. "But their name sours my mouth. Let us eat and enjoy our reward." He led the way to where everyone else was settling down near the fires to be served by six of the followers.

Josiah and Bartholomew maneuvered Jennifer between them and Fargo watched the strain it placed on her natural good manners. He sat down at the outside of the long group and looked up as the small, lithe form appeared with a plate.

"Asa," he said, and the girl smiled and sat down beside him, folding herself with a quick, gliding movement, the buckskin skirt rolling up to show rounded knees and the line of firm, graceful thighs.

"Why do you come through the forest, Fargo?" she asked, and her black eyes danced. "You told Josiah you were searchers."

"Josiah tell you to ask that?"

"He did not have to. It is something he will expect me to find out for him."

"You one of Josiah's wives, Asa?"

"No, I'm nobody's wife yet," the girl said, tossing him a small smile and a sidelong glance. "But you have not answered my question. What do you search for?"

"Not what. Who," Fargo told her. "A man whose horse's hoofprints say came this way."

"Frank Tupper," Asa said, and Fargo saw her pretty face harden.

"Then he was here," Fargo said.

"He was here and he has left," Asa said.

"How long ago?" Fargo questioned.

"Perhaps three, four days ago. I don't remember exactly."

"Then we'll go after him, come morning," Fargo said.

"No, not till you stay a spell," she said. "Josiah will insist on that. You must stay, watch, relax, and let the spirit have time to find its way inside you."

"The spirit?"

"The spirit that will let you join us and stay. He made Frank Tupper do it. You must, too," she said, and her hand closed around his arm. With another quick, gliding movement, she pulled herself against him. "I would like you to join us. You would like it, too. I would see to that," she murmured, and he heard the soft purr that came into her voice. The top of the buckskin shirt moved enough to let him glimpse the curve of high, smallish breasts.

"I don't think you've got your mind on things of the spirit, Asa," Fargo remarked.

"The spirit is in the flesh. You can't separate them." She smiled and he nodded at the reply.

"What if I say we can't stay?" Fargo said. "What if we just leave, come morning?"

"You will never get through the great forest bog," she said. "Not without our help, my help. You will die if you try it on your own."

"The great forest bog?" he echoed.

"It stretches for miles and miles. Many have tried. None have made it,' she said. "Unless they know the way."

"And you know the way," Fargo said, and she nodded. "We could go around this great bog," he said.

"It stretches in all directions. You would lose weeks going around it," she said.

"We'll talk some more tomorrow," Fargo said.

She was on her feet in one quick motion, her smile both mischievous and sensual. "Tomorrow," she said, scooped his plate up, and was gone, melting in among the other women who were clearing up after the meal. He sat back, a smile edging his lips. Asa had been an intriguing little package, to say the least. He didn't like the idea of wasting days, but she might well make the delay worthwhile, he mused. Besides, Frank Tupper had stayed for a spell. Maybe there was more she could tell about him. Fargo swept the thoughts aside and decided not to make decisions until morning. He rose as Bartholomew came toward him.

"We have told the rest of your people they can use the empty shack at the end of the camp, or any of our people will make room for them," the man said.

"Much obliged. I'll sleep outside," Fargo said.

Bartholomew nodded and walked away. The large clearing suddenly became almost still as everyone disappeared into the huts and cabins.

Fargo stood as Jennifer strode toward him.

"I want to leave here tomorrow morning," she snapped.

"Now, that might not be in the cards," he said.

"I know. I heard the same thing that little wildcat was giving you, all about the great bog," Jennifer said. "Well, bog or no bog, I'm getting out of here. This place gives me the creeps. They give me the creeps."

"The climate too spiritual for you, honey?" Fargo commented, and saw her eyes shoot gray fire at him.

"I watched her with you. Spiritual?" Jennifer snapped.

Fargo thought about giving Asa's answer and decided against it. "We'll talk more tomorrow. Get some sleep now," he said, and brought his sleeping bag back from the Ovaro.

"No wrist ropes tonight?" Jennifer frowned.

"There's no place you can run from here," Fargo said. "You know that, too."

"You could be underestimating me," she challenged.

"I could be. Then you'd be a lot dumber than I think you are," he said.

She tightened her lips, walked to her horse, and took her nightclothes from the traveling sack. He had undressed and lay on the bedroll when she returned. With surprise, he saw that she wore only the nightgown as she settled herself onto the blanket not far from where he lay.

"Tossing modesty to the wind?" Fargo asked.

"I feel safe in such a spiritual climate," she said frostily.

He smiled as he watched her pull the blanket over most of herself. But her rounded, bare shoulders remained in view, as did the lovely curve of her high, full breasts under the nightgown. Fargo closed his eyes and Jennifer's words revolved inside him. These welcoming, spiritual people made him uneasy also. There was an air of quiet fanaticism just under the surface, a simmering darkness that hinted at evil. But there was Asa. He'd stand a little fanaticism for a little something else. He'd make no decisions yet, he grunted, and let sleep come to him.

4

"Where are you going?"

Fargo finished buckling his gun belt and turned to where Jennifer looked up at him from the blanket in the first light of dawn. He thought he had dressed quietly enough but he'd plainly been wrong. "Riding," he said. "Be back soon. Get some more sleep for yourself."

"No. I'm going with you," she said, and flung the blanket back.

"Keep it low. Don't wake the whole place up," he muttered.

Her high, full breasts bounced as she strode to the gray filly, her ass narrow and flat yet somehow still sinuous beneath the nightgown. She dressed behind the horse and followed his example as he led the Ovaro out of the camp. He mounted up when they were a dozen yards into the woods and made his way through the twisted trees that were little more than gray shapes in the early dawn.

When he felt the soil grow more moist under the Ovaro's hooves, he reined up and stared at the terrain ahead. The trees were spaced far enough apart to let the new dawn enter; a low layer of mist rose from the soil. Asa had been right. The great forest bog stretched in all directions. He could smell it more than see it, and his lips grew tight. Weaving in and out among the trees, the giant bog stretched far in all directions, the low mist layer seemingly endless.

"It all looks the same to me," Jennifer said. "Just moist soil and trees."

"That's the danger of it," Fargo said.

As she peered ahead with him, the dawn swept away more of the layer of mist and left the tangle of twisted trees. "I don't think there's any damn bog at all," Jennifer said. She flung herself from the saddle and began to march forward.

"Stop, goddammit," Fargo snapped, but she kept marching forward. He pulled his lariat from where it hung on the saddle, twirled it twice, and sent it spinning through the air. It landed around Jennifer. He yanked her to a halt and began to pull her back to him. She turned and didn't resist. Triumph registered in her face.

"I was perfectly fine," she said as he reeled her back to the horse. "I could've gone on. There is no giant bog. That's a story made up to keep people here and try to get converts."

"There's a bog, dammit," Fargo said as he loosened the lasso from around her. "You were lucky. You hit on a firm place. We've been riding on damp, moist soil most of yesterday afternoon. That means water underground, a lot of water to spread out that far." She continued to regard him with skepticism. "Get on your horse. We're going back We'll need them to show us the way through."

"You're going to stick to believing about the bog, are you?"

"You're damn right," Fargo snapped. "Besides, there's more to learn about Frank Tupper."

"And about Asa," Jennifer sniffed as she climbed onto the dark-gray filly and rode back with him.

"You're sounding jealous," Fargo said.

"Ridiculous. I just don't like to be played for a

fool, not by them and not by you," she returned. "You want to cozy up to that little wildcat because you think you can get her in your bedroll."

"I want to cozy up to her to see what she knows and get her to help us out of here," Fargo said. He heard her derisive snort.

The camp was waking as he rode in with Jennifer and he beckoned to Abe Tollner. "We may have to stay a few days," he said. "These people can be of help or they can be trouble."

"Whatever you say," Tollner answered. "We're enjoying ourselves. Some of these womenfolk are right friendly and the food's very good."

Fargo nodded and watched Tollner hurry away as Josiah emerged from a nearby cabin and greeted him expansively.

"Breakfast first. Then morning lessons. I hope you'll join us for both, Fargo," the man said.

"Why not?" Fargo smiled. "Listening never hurt any."

"That's all we ask, friend," Josiah said.

"But what if the spirit doesn't move inside us? What if we listen and decide to move on?" Fargo asked, keeping his tone casual.

"We would be sorrowed and ask the Lord's understanding," Josiah said, and Fargo nodded. He was unsatisfied with the answer, but men such as Josiah often spoke with lofty indirectness and he decided not to press further.

Breakfast was eminently satisfying—bacon, hotcakes, and good coffee—and as the others all gathered in a big circle around Josiah, Fargo saw two of the women had Jennifer between them. She cast a glance about, found him, and glared at the smile he tossed her. He sat down at the edge of the circle and the small form appeared beside him as quietly as a lynx on the prowl. Asa sat against him and he felt the warmth of her even through the buckskin outfit. She sat quietly and listened beside him as Josiah spoke about Joseph Smith and the principles of the new kingdom, of the privilege of being a Mormon and the responsibilities of bringing the message to the world. He was a fire-and-brimstone preacher and the followers rose up in fervor with his exhortations. But when he came to the rift between themselves and the followers of Brigham Young, their fervor took on a vengeful edge. It stayed as he preached about those who turned their backs on the spirit and the truth. When he finished, Fargo felt the uneasiness return to him.

"Don't let Josiah's preaching bother you, Fargo," he heard Asa say.

He turned to her in surprise. "You're pretty damn sharp, girl," he said.

"I've seen it bother others." She smiled and rose with him. "Walk with me," she said.

"Wait," he said, and moved forward to where Jennifer continued to work at being polite as the two women showed her a piece of their embroidery work.

She saw him approach and detached herself. "I want out of this place," she hissed.

"My way, in my time," he said. "Don't do anything stupid. I won't be far away."

Her eyes flicked to where Asa waited. "But you'll be busy," she sniffed.

"Not the way you mean. I told you, I think she can help us. I want to make sure," he said.

Jennifer turned from him with a glance of disdain and disbelief. He watched as she walked toward one of the cabins with the two women, and then he returned to where Asa waited. Her hand curled inside his, a little ball of warmth, and she led him out of the camp to a thick cluster of tangled trees that rose up above the north end of the clearing. She sat down on a bed of elf-cap moss and pulled him beside her.

"You have things to ask me, Fargo," she said. "I have things to ask you."

"A few," he admitted, and she lay back, lifted one leg languorously, and he felt the throbbing of her as her black eyes held him. "You first," he said.

"I will help you if you will help me," she said, and his frown questioned. She sat up and her hand rose, pressed against his chest. "Other eyes may be watching. This is not the time or place to say all of it. But I will take you through the giant bog if you take me with you."

He knew his brows lifted in surprise. "You want to leave here?" he asked.

She nodded and sat up, crossing the lithe, firm young legs. "I want to leave. You can take me. You won't regret it," she said.

"I thought you were a follower, one of Josiah's believers," Fargo said.

"I have my reasons," she said. "I'll tell you when we're far away from here." She rose abruptly. "Let us go back. I don't want suspicions aroused."

He pushed to his feet and began to walk back with her. "How did you come here in the first place, Asa?" he asked.

"I joined Josiah back in Ohio. I wanted to run away. I hated my home, my stepfather," she said.

"And now you want to run away again?" Fargo said, and she nodded. "Did you ask Frank Tupper to take you?" he slid at her.

"Maybe," she said. "But he told me he was running and he had to go alone. I helped him through the bog." She pressed his arm as they started down into the camp. "Tonight, behind the last hut at the far end of the cabin, after everyone is asleep . . .

73

I'll wait for you. We'll talk more then. You won't be sorry you came."

"All right." He nodded, and strolled slowly as she hurried off. He saw Josiah beckon to her when she reached the center of the camp, and the man walked off with her. Fargo frowned and again felt the uncertainty inside himself. Asa continued to be a provocative surprise.

He found a tree trunk that let him overlook the camp and he sat down against it. He watched the busyness of the community, everyone doing some task, not a soul standing idle. They even had Abe Tollner and his boys working along, fixing fires, scraping hides, carrying water. Yet he felt a strange air to the camp. He'd not seen military compounds this ordered and busy. It was as though they had substituted work for everything else in the world— for thinking, relaxing, enjoying. But then work and self-discipline were their enjoyment, he reminded himself. But something still bothered him and suddenly the word flashed in his mind: *zealots*. They were zealots in their beliefs, zealots in their work, in their self-discipline, in everything.

Perhaps that was necessary for some, he mused, and as his eyes scanned the camp, he realized that Jennifer wasn't anywhere he could see. He rose and walked down into the heart of the camp, peered through the open doors of some of the cabins, and saw they were empty.

Josiah and Bartholomew came by and Fargo nodded to the two men. "I'm looking for Jennifer," he said.

"We have not seen her since the morning lesson," Josiah said, and walked on.

Fargo felt the apprehension crawl up the back of his neck and he hurried to where Abe Tollner helped two women stir the stew in a huge black kettle.

"Where's the judge's daughter?" he asked, and the man shrugged.

"Don't have any idea. She's your charge," Tollner answered.

Fargo swore under his breath and strode away. The gray filly was tethered beside the Ovaro, but Jennifer was gone. She had slipped from camp on foot. That meant she wasn't trying to flee. She'd gone off to prove to him that she was right about the bog.

He swore as he ran, pausing at the Ovaro to take the lariat, and continuing on foot. She'd be well into the bog by now, too damn well into it, he cursed. His only chance was on foot, and he broke into a long, loping trot as he picked up her footprints. The lower layer of mists had burned off in the afternoon warmth and the vast tangle of trees stretched ahead of him. Some formed their own clusters and others reached up alone, a vast labyrinth that beckoned in every direction and concealed the death that lurked within its grip. He felt the softness in the ground, slowed his stride, and saw Jennifer's footprints turn, veer sharply to the left.

He followed and drew to a halt and half-leapt backward as his left foot sank down to the ankle. He dropped to one knee and peered forward, a terrible pain knotting his insides. She'd had too much time. She could be sucked down by now, anywhere, anyplace. The great bog existed, all through the land that all but surrounded him. He strained his eyes and swept the ground with a slow stare and suddenly he halted and heard the gasp that escaped his lips. Against a decayed log, her head was still visible, her eyes closed. He rose and called out, softly first, then louder. He saw the exhaustion in her face. She had struggled and fought, perhaps for hours, against the sucking grasp that inexorably pulled her down into the mud. She had finally stopped struggling, defeat overwhelming.

"Jennifer," he shouted again, and saw her eyes come open. "Jennifer," he called. "Over here." He waited, saw her turn her head, and he held the lariat in his hand. He couldn't throw it, not yet. The only spot it could land was around her neck and the rope would strangle her as he tried to pull her free. "Can you see me? Do you hear me?" he asked as she stared almost blankly across the distance toward him. He watched her eyes, saw the flicker come into them, and called out again. "Pull your arm free, Jennifer. Can you pull your arm free?" he shouted, and then again, "Your arm. Pull your arm up."

Her eyes flickered once more as he saw her lift her head. Slowly, with what was probably her last remaining grain of strength, she managed to lift one arm out of the sucking ooze.

"Good, that's it, good," Fargo encouraged. "Lift it over your head, Jennifer. Hold your arm up. That's it . . . high as you can."

Slowly, every moment a tremendous exercise of will over exhaustion, she raised her arm upward, managing to hold it almost straight into the air. Fargo rose, took aim, and sent the lariat whirling through the air. The lasso came down over her, partially hitting against her head but with the main part of the noose settling over her upraised arm. Fargo yanked it tight at once, and as her arm fell, he had the noose secured around her upper arm. He began to pull, slowly and carefully at first, and he felt the resistance as the bog refused to willingly relinquish its prey. He dropped to one knee for balance and to keep the rope taut and low as he pulled again. Slowly, Jennifer's other arm came free and she managed to wrap both hands around the lariat. He pulled again, a steady pressure that kept her from sinking down into the ooze, and inch by inch Jennifer slid toward him, her hands desperately locked around the lariat.

He knew the pull on the lower part of her body had to be tremendous as the thick ooze of the bog clung. He felt the strain of his own back muscles. When his shoulder and arm muscles began to burn with pain, he dared to halt for a moment but his eyes stayed on Jennifer, watching as the thick ooze held her in place for a few moments. When he saw her start to sink again, he began to pull at once and the instant of panic left her eyes. Dusk descended, then the darkness, and finally the faint light of a high moon that filtered down, and he still had yards of distance between himself and Jennifer. He paused again, drew in deep drafts of air. He felt the burning strain of every muscle of his body now, and he began to wonder if he had enough strength left to bring her in. He shook away the thought angrily and let the anger summon up renewed strength as he began to pull again. But suddenly, as Jennifer drew closer, the heavy, clinging, sucking ooze thinned out and he felt her moving more easily. Not unlike a man seeing the light at the end of the tunnel, he increased his pulling, ignored the pain of his body, and finally he could reach out and grasp her hand. With a final pull he drew her onto the firm ground and fell back to lie gasping for breath.

Finally he pushed himself onto one elbow and looked at Jennifer. She still lay facedown, the thick ooze covering her from her neck to her toes, but she was breathing evenly and she turned her head to him. "I'm sorry," she murmured. "I should've listened to you."

"Goddamn right about that," Fargo growled, sitting up beside her. "Let's see if you can walk," he said as he lifted her to her feet.

She took a hesitant step, swayed, took another, and nodded. "I can walk, but all this ooze on me weighs a ton."

"There's fresh, clear water, a good-size stream, near the camp. That's where they get all their water. You can wash it off there," he told her, and holding her elbow, he walked with her along the firm ground. He circled around the camp area to the stream and Jennifer sank down beside it. "I'll help you get your clothes off," Fargo offered, and she shook her head firmly.

"I'll manage myself," she said.

"Modesty no matter what?" he grunted.

"I can do it myself," she said. "But I'll need something dry to wear. Can you bring it to me?"

"I guess so," he said. "You stay here until I come back, understand?"

"I will, believe me," she said. "I'm too exhausted to go anywhere."

He turned and hurried from her at a half-trot, reached the camp, and made his way through the silent grounds to the last hut and circled behind it. He saw Asa rise and come toward him.

"I was about to leave," she said with some annoyance.

"There was an accident," he said. "Can we talk tomorrow night? Same place, same time?"

"Was it the girl?" Asa asked.

"Yes. She was stupid," Fargo said.

Asa's smile held an edge of triumph and of mockery. "Tomorrow night, promise?" she said.

"Promise," he echoed, and suddenly she stood on tiptoes. Her lips pressed against his and he felt her tongue slide slowly across her mouth and then retreat.

"To help you keep your promise," she murmured as she pulled back with a sly smile.

"It'll do that." He grinned.

She turned and darted into the darkness like a wild creature seeking safety.

Fargo, a furrow staying on his brow, walked slowly to the Ovaro, took a towel from his saddlebag and then a blouse and skirt from the sack hanging from the gray filly.

Jennifer was waiting behind a tree when he returned and poked her head out. He tossed her the towel, then the clothes, and when she stepped out, she was still drying her hair with the towel.

"Thank you," she murmured, and returned the towel to him. "I feel drained, absolutely exhausted. I could sleep for a week."

"You've till morning," he said, and walked back to the camp with her, where she sank down onto the ground at once. He tossed her a blanket and she covered herself with it while she wriggled out of the blouse.

"There are things I'd like to say, but I'd rather wait till morning," she offered.

He shrugged but his eyes were cold as they peered at her. "I'm wondering if I ought to go back to tying you," he said.

"There's no need. That's a promise," she said. "I keep my word."

"You'd better," he growled, and began to pull off his clothes. When he lay down atop his bedroll, he felt the muscles of his back and shoulders tremble as they finally relaxed and he saw Jennifer was only an arm's length away, her eyes still open, watching him. "Thought you were exhausted," he muttered.

She let her eyes close but he heard the whispered words come from her lips. "Thank you," she murmured. He grunted and let the soothing balm of sleep sweep over his aching body.

The night stayed silent and the tiredness in him let him sleep later than he normally would, and he woke when the sounds of the camp came to him. He rose, washed with the water from his canteen, and let Jennifer sleep till she woke on her own. "See you at breakfast," he said, and sauntered down into the center of camp.

Abe Tollner eyed him as he approached. "You find her?" the man said.

Fargo nodded and accepted a tin cup of coffee from one of the women who paused beside him. " 'Morning, and bless you, friend," she said, and went on her way.

Jennifer finally came down when breakfast was nearly over but in time to share in the last of the hotcakes and coffee. Two of the women went to her and filled the morning with chatter until Josiah appeared for the morning lesson. They kept Jennifer between them, Fargo noticed, all done with a happy firmness. He sat down at the perimeter of the circle and listened as he had the morning before. Josiah's preaching was more heavily sprinkled with quotations from Joseph Smith's teachings on the power of right than the previous morning. The followers were quicker to join in with amens and hosannas.

But finally the lesson ended and he saw Asa watching him. He waited but she did not come to stand beside him at all, so he made his way back to the edge of the camp where the Ovaro was tethered. He began to saddle the horse and had just finished when Jennifer came up.

"Going somewhere?" she asked.

"Back to the edge of the bog," he said.

"What in heaven for?" She frowned.

"Curiosity," he said, and she sniffed.

"I know better than that. You've a reason," she said, "May I come?"

"I'd imagine you had enough of that place for a spell," he said in surprise.

"I'd still like to come," she said.

He shrugged and waited until she climbed onto the dark-gray filly. She rode quietly beside him for the short distance to the edge of the bog. He halted the horse and let his eyes scan the tangle of twisted trees and the innocent-appearing terrain. He slid from the pinto and squatted on the ground, his eyes narrowed as he peered over the low layer of mist. He studied the ground for minutes as Jennifer dismounted and waited, watched his probing gaze. Finally he broke off and rose to his feet.

"What'd you find out?" she asked.

"I'm not sure," he said.

"What were you looking for?"

"Things."

"Things you're not sure about."

"That's right." He laughed.

Her face grew serious and she rested one hand against his chest. "About yesterday, there's little to say except that I'm grateful for what you did," she said. "You see, not looking a gift horse in the mouth."

"Good," he grunted.

"But for the first time I have a real understanding of what it must have been like to be a temple virgin," she said.

"A what?" Fargo frowned.

"A temple virgin," she said. "In ancient Rome, virgins were sometimes sacrificed to the gods. Especially picked, they were kept in the temple, pampered and powdered, given the very best of everything, and looked after and protected so no harm would come to them, all so they could be sacrificed when the time came."

He allowed a slow smile at her analogy. "This is different," he said.

"Not really," she said firmly.

"It's different. There are two maybes here," he said, and she frowned back. "Maybe you won't have to be sacrificed and maybe you're no virgin."

Her eyes narrowed. "Well, you'll find out one answer when the time comes," she said.

"Or both," he remarked, and she shot a glare at him.

"Hardly likely," she sniffed.

"Let's ride some. Stay behind me," he said, and began to move the pinto in a wide circle along the periphery of the bog. It was risky, he realized, the bog able to extend unseen at any point, and he rode slowly and let the horse move by its own instincts. He continued to peer into the terrain while staying alert to the horse's every step, ready to pull back at an instant. Finally, the day beginning to close down, he had Jennifer back out ahead of him and turned away from the vast, uncharted, treacherous terrain.

"You have your little talk with Asa yet?" Jennifer asked as she came to ride beside him.

"Not yet," he said.

"She's practically wild. There's something about her that frightens me," Jennifer said. "She's like a feral cat, on the lookout for prey."

"She's not like the others," Fargo said. "She doesn't have all that discipline. She's not the same kind of believer."

"She's the same. She just wears a different mask," Jennifer said.

"I don't see that," Fargo said.

"You're obviously too interested in something else," she sniffed with disapproval.

"I'm just going to draw her out, find out what she can tell me about Frank Tupper, and get her to help us out of here. I told you that," Fargo said.

Jennifer cast a long glance at him. "I'd like to believe you."

"Take my word for it," Fargo said as they reached the camp. He tethered the horses and unsaddled both as Jennifer walked on to where supper was being readied. After the meal, Josiah gave his evening sermon by the firelight and Fargo returned to the slope at the edge of the camp as night settled in.

Jennifer came to pause for a moment beside him. "I'm still terribly tired."

"Not surprised. Another good sleep ought to help," he said.

She disappeared into the trees to change. When she returned she pulled up the blanket he had set out, and lay down. He undressed to only his trousers and watched her eyes close and sleep come to her.

He waited until the rest of the camp had grown silent before he rose and, bare-chested, moved quietly around the edge of the cabins until he reached the last one at the other end. He halted, frowned into the pale light, and saw the small shape appear and move toward him on silent steps.

Asa stopped before him, her eyes moving across his powerfully muscled chest with undisguised pleasure. "This way," she whispered, and her hand curled inside his again and he followed her to a slope of thick silky fork moss where she folded herself onto the ground and drew him down beside her. Her black eyes roamed over him again and he felt the sensuous throbbing of her as she slowly rubbed first one leg and then the other against the soft moss, the gesture languorous, feline in its fluid beauty. "I want to go with you, Fargo," she said.

"Tell me more about Frank Tupper first," Fargo said. "He told you he was running. Did he say where he was going?"

"He named a place, the foot of King's Peak," she said.

"He tell you why he was going there?" Fargo questioned.

"He said he had family there, two brothers," Asa said.

"He tell you anything else?" Fargo pressed.

"No. I didn't like him much." Asa's hand reached out to trace a lazy line across his chest. "He was nothing like you," she murmured. Her hand stole around the back of his neck, a soft but firm pressure as she pulled his mouth down to hers. "I want you to be happy with me, Fargo," she murmured, and her mouth opened for his at once, soft yet firm, and her tongue darted out instantly. She moved against him and he felt her hand moving along his body, halting at the top of his Levi's, fumbling at buttons. He reached down, gently pushed her away, and pulled the trousers off.

Asa sat up, wrapped both arms around herself, and flung the buckskin top over her head. She smiled in delight as she sat very straight in front of him and enjoyed his enjoyment of her as he took in small but perfectly shaped breasts, olive skin smooth with dark brown-pink nipples standing erect, each surrounded by a light-brown circle. She had square shoulders and a torso absolutely without fat, yet she was without sharp angles, everything flowing smoothly into everything else. She lifted her hips and yanked and the buckskin skirt came off and he saw lithe, supple legs, a flat belly, and a surprisingly abundant, tangled black nap. She was a small girl yet everything matched perfectly, shoulders, breasts, hips, legs, all of a piece. She could have been an elf were it not for the throbbing darkness she exuded, which made her a thing more of wildness than spriteliness.

She came to him, her black eyes burning, and when her sharply pointed breasts touched his skin, she cried out, a sharp sound, something between a gasp and a laugh but fashioned of pure tactile delight. Her nipples already firm against him, she twisted her body, pushing the very abundant black nap hard against him and crying out. He lay down with her as she flipped onto her back and he brought his mouth down around one small, piquant breast and sucked gently.

"Oh, Jesus . . . yes, Jesus, yes . . . oh, oh, ayieee, ayieee," Asa cried out. He felt her torso twisting, her lean legs flailing from one side to the other. He continued to pull gently, moved to the other breast, and Asa's hands pulled themselves up and down his muscled body, clutching at his buttocks, digging into his back. "Oh, God . . . yes, so fine, so so fine, aaaayyyyeeeee," Asa cried out, a long, rising sound that trailed off and rose again. He drew his mouth from her breasts, looked down at her and saw the feverish burning in her black eyes, her thick black hair a jet halo around her head as his hand moved down over her concave abdomen to press into the thick, tangled curliness.

Her hand flew down to cover his, push him down to the bottom of the black tangle, and he felt the nap already wet with her flowing. "Yes, yes, yes, Fargo," Asa murmured, each word ending in a harsh gasp. "Touch me, feel me, take me, oh, Jesus, for you, for you, for you," she gasped. He moved to cup his hand around the warm, wet portal, and Asa half-screamed and her body arched backward. He moved his hand, probed, touching the deliquescent walls. Asa moaned and her body leapt under him.

He felt her hands pulling on his thighs, trying to bring his hotly throbbing maleness over her, and when he rolled onto her and pressed against her pubic mound, she cried out with a scream of ecstasy. Her lean legs flung themselves apart and she seemed to buck under him as she clutched at him, entreated with flesh and spirit, her head thrown back, her piquant breasts thrusting upward.

He came to her, slid into her warm flowing, and she began to thrust and push against him with wild, feverish motions. Asa cried out, gasped, swallowed words, half-screamed, half-moaned, and he felt the clutching contractions of her around him, her legs tightening against him with his every thrust, the warm, flowing glove of vibrant flesh tight around him. He felt himself being carried up by her thrashing wildness.

Suddenly her eyes came open wide and her hands became fists that pounded against his back. "Now, now, Jesus, now . . . the coming, coming . . . everything . . . ah, ah . . . aaiiiii," Asa screamed out, and Fargo felt himself explode with her as her lean, tight body shook and quivered against him, all of her a throbbing, white-hot wire of flesh and muscle until finally, as the moment of moments vanished, she uttered a whimper of despair and fell away from him, tiny sobs coming to rack her body, and he lay down over her until she became still.

"It shouldn't end," Asa murmured, resentment in her voice. "It shouldn't."

"It's got to," Fargo said. "It was planned that way."

Asa brought her black eyes to focus on him. "Yes, it is planned, all of it, everything planned for us," she said, and brought her arms around his neck. "It will be wonderful now, Fargo. You'll see. You won't be sorry you've come to Asa."

"You expect we'll sneak out by night," Fargo said as he began to pull on trousers. "You want to start making plans now?"

"No, plans will come tomorrow," Asa said, and she rose and pressed her still-nude body against him. "This was just a beginning," she murmured. He held her for a moment. Her throbbing wildness could turn into a kind of childlike simplicity with startling abruptness, he noted again. Asa was indeed a strange little creature, and when she moved back, her smile was almost serene. "Tomorrow," she said as she stepped into her buckskins. She vanished into the dark before he had a chance to turn away.

He made his way around the edge of the camp and returned to his bedroll. As he stretched out, he saw Jennifer push up on one elbow under the blanket. "I presume you had your whatever," she said icily.

He decided to ignore her barb. "We had our talk. Things are settled. I'll tell you more tomorrow, after breakfast." He closed his eyes and drew sleep around himself.

5

Next morning Jennifer walked down to breakfast beside him and sat nearby when Josiah began his morning lesson. Fargo found Asa, not far from Josiah, and she caught his glance and returned a wide, happy smile.

The sermon was heavy on obeying the real truth and not those who distorted it, such as Brigham Young. "There is talk of making that man governor of the territory and he revels in it. What more proof is needed that he is of the material not the spiritual?" Josiah asked his audience and went on with an impassioned scriptural lesson. When he finally ended he took a step back and bestowed a benevolent smile on his followers.

"And now, a special announcement, one that makes my heart glow with happiness. A new follower has joined our happy family," he said, and Fargo felt the frown immediately dig into his brow. He caught Abe Tollner's eye and the man shrugged back at him from where he sat between two of the women. Fargo brought his eyes back to Josiah as the man raised his voice another notch. "Last night, the man called Fargo joined with our own Asa. As you all know, a joining of the flesh is a joining of the spirit, an acceptance of the body is an acceptance of the faith. And so, in the spirit of our community of those who believe in the mission of

Joseph Smith and the Latter-day Saints, our brother Fargo has become one of us. He has lain with our Asa and she with him and together they will be part of us."

Fargo stared in shock and astonishment. He half-turned to Jennifer and saw the flare in her gray eyes.

"Talking?" she hissed. "I don't know why I ever believed you in the first place."

"Now, hold a minute. I didn't bargain for this," Fargo began, and cut off further words as three of the men appeared behind him, led by Bartholomew.

"We will take your gun, Fargo," Bartholomew said, and Fargo saw the other three men held rifles. One reached down and pulled the Colt from its holster. "New members are not permitted to carry firearms," Bartholomew explained calmly. "Not till they have been with us for six months and we can see the spirit is deep inside them."

Fargo said nothing, seething inside, and the men walked off with his gun. His eyes found Asa and she waved happily at him.

Jennifer pushed to her feet and stalked away. "Bastard," he heard her hiss.

"Welcome and bless you," a woman called to Fargo.

"Bless you, Fargo," another said cheerily.

Fargo's voice lifted as he called after Bartholomew. "What are you going to do with my Colt?" he asked. "I've had it a long time."

"It will be perfectly safe in my cabin," Bartholomew called back, and went on.

Fargo, his face stone, strode across the camp to where Asa waited, the serene smile still on her face. He took her by the elbow and began to march her to one side, his words muttered through lips that barely moved. "You've some tall explaining to do, honey," he said.

"You're hurting me," she protested, and he relaxed his grip on her arm.

"Why?" he bit out.

"Why what, Fargo?" She blinked.

"Why this, goddammit? Why'd you tell him?" Fargo rasped.

"It was what had to be done," Asa said calmly.

"You better have some plan to go with all this," Fargo hissed.

"Plan? It was all planned, everything that has happened," Asa answered.

"You wanted me to take you out of here?" He frowned.

"Only if we couldn't stay here together," she said. "But we can now."

"You little bitch. You set it all up," Fargo growled.

"It was meant to be, Fargo. You came here because you were meant to come, don't you see? And I was here waiting for you. You'll be happy here, you'll see," Asa said.

Fargo heard the calm conviction in her voice. She manipulated, she maneuvered, but she also believed, he realized. In her book, the flesh was in the service of the spirit.

"You really think you can keep me here?" he asked, and heard the incredulousness in his voice.

But she only smiled again, the same serenely confident smile, and came against him. She pressed her breasts hard against him while her leg rubbed against the inner part of his thigh with sinuous provocativeness. "Of course."

He held back the answer that leapt to his tongue. Two could pay at manipulation. "Of course," he echoed, and added a note of acceptance. "What happens tonight?" he asked, and cupped her face with his hand. "Do we join again tonight? I'd like that."

"The last hut at the end of the camp will be ours," Asa said. "I'll wait for you there."

"Tell me, what happens to the others who came with me? Do they go if they want to?" he asked.

"Probably not. The girl can be made to believe and bear children for us. The community needs children. They are the seeds of tomorrow. The men can also be touched with the spirit in time," Asa said.

"And if they're not?" Fargo pressed.

"That will be for Josiah to decide," she said. "But the community cannot allow those who might harm it to exist."

"Naturally," Fargo said.

"Tonight," Asa said with that special combination of provocativeness and serenity he had come to realize was deep inside her.

Fargo watched her hurry off to join the other women, who had begun to tan a moose hide. He walked through the camp to the other end where Jennifer sat near her gray filly, knees drawn up, arms clasped around her legs. She refused to look at him as he sat down near her.

"You all steamed up because I got taken or got laid?" he asked.

Her eyes flashed gray fire as she threw a glance at him. "They're one and the same," she snapped. "You deserve staying here. You were so quick to enjoy yourself. Now you'll be paying the price. As for me, I'm getting out of here."

"You can't get through the bog. You found that out," he said.

"I'm not trying that again, I'm going back the way we came. I'll find my way somehow," Jennifer said, anger and determination in her face.

"Maybe and maybe not. It doesn't matter," Fargo said. "They won't let you out of here. They'll be watching you."

"How do you know that?" She frowned.

"I was told as much," he said. "And if you did get out and started back, they'd come after you. The only way out is to find the way through the bog. They won't come chasing through there after us. It's too dangerous."

"Us?" Jennifer snapped.

"That's right. You don't think I'm going to stay here, do you?"

"I don't think you've much choice."

He let a grim snort escape his lips. "You bed down here as usual tonight, only keep your clothes on," he said.

She studied his face with a narrowed glance. "If they'll be watching me, they'll certainly be watching you. How do you expect to get free?"

"That's my problem," he said.

Her eyes stayed on him, probing. "I believe you mean it," Jennifer said slowly. "But then I believed you when you said you were only going to talk to her."

"I was. Can I help it if I'm too sympathetic in some situations?" he said blandly.

"Too sympathetic?" she snorted. "Too damn eager, that's what."

He rose and her eyes on him saw his jaw harden. "Doesn't matter now. What matters is you go through the rest of the day as usual. Play it out, you understand?"

"What if you don't show up tonight?" she asked.

"I'll be here before the night's out. You just be ready," he growled, and walked away. His eyes swept the long, busy camp area and he saw Abe Tollner detach himself from his men and start toward him. He could just leave with Jennifer, Fargo knew, and let Tollner and his men shift for themselves. He'd never wanted them along in the first place. This would be his chance to get rid of them. But he'd be sealing their death warrants. Asa's roundabout answers had told him that much, and he halted as Tollner confronted him.

"What are you trying to pull off, Fargo?" Tollner demanded, his voice tight. "I never figured you for staying on here."

"Neither did I," Fargo said, and saw surprise come into Tollner's eyes. "I was tricked, dry-gulched by pussy, you might say."

"So what happens to us now?"

"Nothing, if you want to stay on."

"Stay on?" Abe frowned. "You crazy? A little friendly feel is enough. We're not staying on. You can have 'em all."

"I'm not staying, either. But these are dangerous people. They're not going to let you walk out."

"What do you figure to do?" Tollner asked.

"Get out of here tonight," Fargo said. "Until then, you play it just as you have been. Stay friendly. You might even ask about becoming a member of the community. They'll be watching me and they'll be watching Jennifer. I don't want them uneasy about you."

"All right, What, then?" Abe pressed.

"You know where I've been bedding down at the other end of camp?" Fargo asked, and Tollner nodded. "Meet me there one hour before dawn. Tell your men to come one by one. No noise."

"One hour before dawn," Tollner repeated.

"That's right. We're going to need light to get through the bog," the Trailsman said. "Now get back and be friendly."

Tollner nodded and sauntered away. He rejoined

his men, spoke to them for a few moments, and then they scattered and made their way through camp, Tollner joining three women cutting up venison for stew.

Fargo spotted Asa with Josiah and another woman as they tried to shore up one end of a cabin where the wood had come apart at the joints. "Mind if I help," he said as he hurried down. "Might as well get into the spirit of things."

"Indeed," Josiah said, and Asa squeezed his arm happily.

Fargo took the far end of the plank they were trying to put in place and, using the strength of his powerful frame, held it aloft while the others used wooden pegs to nail it on securely. Two more shorter lengths of log finished the job and the cabin was firm and secure again.

Asa put her arm around his waist and her small form clung to him. "You see, I told you he would not hold back," she said to Josiah, and the man nodded approvingly.

"I am pleased," he said. "In time, Fargo, you may take another wife. This is our custom, so our community will produce children."

Fargo smiled down at Asa and hugged her to him. "Right now I'll stick to Asa," he said, and Josiah nodded.

Asa walked with him and Fargo followed as Josiah made his way to the center of the camp, where the supper meal was being readied. When the meal was served Fargo saw Jennifer sit with three of the women and he watched her chatter away. She was cooperating, he noted with satisfaction. His eyes found Tollner and his men spread around the semicircle, ostensibly enjoying themselves.

The meal ended, Josiah gave his evening lesson

and Asa left to join the other women as they cleared away the utensils.

Dark lay over the camp as the fires burned down and Fargo sauntered to where the Ovaro was tethered beside Jennifer's gray. He took his lariat from the saddle, hung it on to his belt, and saw Jennifer arrive. He also saw two of the women with her.

She halted beside him. "This is Tabatha and Priscilla," she introduced. "They invited me to sleep in their cabin but I told them I prefer sleeping in the open so they decided to join me." Jennifer caught his faint nod, he saw as he smiled at the two women. Both were large-framed women, a very definite firmness just under the cordial smiles they returned.

"You'll be going to Asa, of course," one said.

"Of course." Fargo smiled. "Sleep well, ladies." He strolled away slowly, casually, pausing in the center of camp to watch Josiah go into the largest of the cabins. Bartholomew's cabin was the next down the line, he had already noted, and he slowly wandered on to the other end of camp where the small hut stood a half-dozen yards from the other dwellings. He halted in surprise as he saw the man with a rifle at his side and two women seated just outside the cabin door.

"Asa is inside waiting for you," one of the women said pleasantly.

Fargo let his eyes move across the trio. "You a guard of honor or just a guard?" he asked.

"We watch over those who are newly joined. It is our custom," one of the women said.

"Another custom." Fargo smiled and went past the three figures and into the cabin. He pushed the door closed behind him and saw two candles affording more than enough light to reveal Asa sitting on a large bearskin rug, cross-legged and naked as a jaybird, her small, piquant breasts pointing upward with their own spicy loveliness.

"The spirit isn't very trusting, is it?" he muttered as he sank down beside her.

"Precautions are not distrust," Asa said. "Satan works in many ways. It will all stop when you have been one with us for a longer time."

They had a serene answer for everything, he realized, and he began to pull off clothes. The door wasn't thick and the three outside would easily hear. Just as well, he smiled inwardly. He might as well enjoy the first part of the night. He shed the last of his clothes and Asa came atop him at once with her quick, catlike movements. She rubbed her large, abundant nap across his groin as she made little sounds of delight. Her eager wanting was no sham, he knew. He felt his own desires respond and he grew thick beneath her, his maleness burgeoning, pressing against her densely covered pubic mound.

"Ayiii . . . ayeeeiiii, oh, Jesus, oh, yes," Asa cried out, lifting her head and shouting as he rose and pressed up against the warm portal. Her knees drew up and she wriggled herself atop him, the thread trying to find the needle, and when she came down atop him, her scream reverberated through the cabin.

"They'll hear outside, you know," he murmured against her cheek.

"Yes, yes, they'll hear and they'll enjoy for us and for themselves. They'll know, they'll understand," she gasped out.

"The flesh serves the spirit," Fargo murmured as she pumped herself atop him.

"Yes, yes," Asa gasped out. "For us all, for us all."

"For them too?" he breathed and she nodded against him as her tight, small rear rose and fell with increasing speed. She pumped ferverishly. He found one small breast, pulled on it, and she screamed in pleasure. She continued to twist her torso, pumping wildly atop him, driving herself down as deeply as she could upon his pulsating spear, which filled her smallness completely. He grasped her rear, one big hand all but covering each small, tight buttock, holding her halfway up as she tried to come down.

"Oh, no, no, let me, let me," Asa cried out, and when he relaxed his grip, she came down upon him with a scream of relief and desire all rolled into one. He let her go on then, her body running away with itself, and he felt his own urgings begin to spiral. When he felt her stiffen, then stretch backward, lifting her head up as her black hair cascaded wildly in all directions, he let himself erupt with her and there was nothing serene or spiritual in her scream of absolute carnality. Finally, when she collapsed over him, he heard her half-sobs of despair again and she moaned into his chest.

He turned her onto her back. "Something added this time, honey," he said, and his fist struck the point of her jaw in a short, sharp blow and Asa's head fell sideways as she went out at once. He rose, silently pulled on trousers and boots, and his gaze swept the hut. He spotted an iron skillet and a small iron pot; he chose the pot and made his way to the door on silent steps. Asa's fevered enthusiasm had seemed to make time fly, but their lovemaking had been more than long enough and he carefully pushed the door open an inch, enough for him to peer outside. He saw the rifle lying on the ground, and a few paces beyond, the three forms entwined. He saw the back of the man's legs as he lay atop one of the women, his trousers down around his ankles. The second woman lay over him, pressed down hard onto him, her bare and ample rear up in the air, and she moved with him, as though trying to help him in his thrustings.

Fargo stole from the hut, put the iron pot down, and picked up the rifle. There was no time for anything but unfeeling harshness, he realized. "Sorry to interrupt," he murmured nonetheless as he yanked the woman on top by the hair and hit her in the jaw with a short left, dropped her to one side, and brought the rifle butt down on the back of the man's head. He went limp and Fargo kicked him aside. The third woman stared up at him, blinking with uncomprehending astonishment before he knocked her out with a short, chopping blow to the jaw.

He dragged the man into the hut first, then the two women, and used their blouses and shirts to make gags and bonds for all three. He used the man's belt to strap his ankles tightly together and wrapped him and one of the woman together so they were all but immovable. He used his lariat to tie Asa's wrists and ankles and one of the women's scarves as a gag for her and the others. They were still all unconscious as he crept from the hut and made his way around to the rear of the cabins until he reached the one that held Bartholomew. Rifle in hand, he pushed the door open carefully as he lay prone on the ground and let his eyes grow used to the darkness inside. He made out the man's heavy-set form at the right of the cabin on a cot; two women slept on palettes nearby.

Fargo scanned the walls until he found the Colt hanging on a peg. He crawled on his hands and knees, inched his way around the walls of the cabin, his eyes flicking from Bartholomew to the two women and back again. He halted when he reached the Colt, carefully lifted it from the peg and slipped it into his holster, paused, and began the slow, silent retracing of steps. He reached the door and the room remained still, only the even sounds of sleep coming from inside. He suppressed a sigh of gratefulness as he crawled into the night air.

He stayed in a crouch as he returned to the hut where he'd left Asa and the others. The man was awake when he reached the hut and Fargo seated himself on the floor and relaxed against the wall. He let the hours go by and Asa was next to wake, her eyes glaring fury at him,. The two women came around soon after and stared over the gags around their mouths, their eyes moving from him to the man, then to Asa and around the circle again.

Fargo reached out and ran his hand over Asa's naked body. She was warm and he discarded the idea of untying her and letting her put on clothes. She was quick, lithe, and furious and he'd take no chances, he decided. He smiled as he saw the man working his arms and wrists in an effort to loosen his bonds.

"Relax," Fargo told him. "The only way you'll get those off is when somebody cuts you loose." He put his head back against the wall of the hut, let himself catnap, and waited for the morning hours to slide by. Finally he rose, adjusted the lariat hanging from his belt, and saw a one-piece, sleeveless brown, shift lying on the floor. He picked it up, pushed it into the ropes around Asa's wrists, and let it dangle there as he lifted her to her feet. "Time to move out," he said. He brought his fist around in a short arc and clipped Asa on the point of the jaw and caught her as she collapsed. He swung her over one shoulder and paused at the door of the cabin to glance back at the three tightly bound and gagged figures. "I'm real sorry I can't stay. I don't know anything much about this Brigham Young and the

Mormons," he said. "but I know that you're a bunch of crazies, and I'm sure he'd think so, too."

He stepped from the hut, paused, swept the camp with a long glance before moving around to the back of the hut and into the trees that circled the camp area. Asa's small form was almost weightless. He hurried through the trees and when he reached the end of the camp, he dropped to one knee and peered through the trees. The two women were still there, one on each side of Jennifer, but he'd expected that. He lowered Asa to the ground alongside a tree trunk and ignored the fury in her black eyes. He crept forward and halted at the edge of the trees. He had to find a way to take over both women at once. One cry from either and it was all over, he knew. Then he saw the figure approach from the side of the slope.

The figure drew closer, and became Abe Tollner. Fargo saw one of the women wake instantly and sit up. The other snapped awake seconds later as Tollner drew to a halt before them.

"What is it you want here?" the nearest woman said, her hair in a bun at the back of her head. "You woke us. We were asleep."

"Came to see Fargo," Tollner said, rushing words a trifle.

"He is with Asa," the woman answered, and Fargo saw Jennifer wake, push up on her elbow.

"I thought maybe they'd both be up here," Tollner said, and took another two steps closer.

"No," the woman said firmly. "Please return to your friends."

"Hell, I just came from there," Tollner said, and took another step.

Fargo saw the woman's arm move and from beneath her full skirt she drew a pistol and leveled it at Tollner. Fargo found himself staring at the pistol, a rotating-barrel percussion pepperbox of the kind he hadn't seen in ten years. But the long cocking spur and the bar hammer marked it as a Stocking and Company piece out of Worcester, Massachusetts. Almost a collector's item, the six barrels could rotate fast enough to blast a mighty big hole in a man, and Tollner had the good sense to halt.

"Go back down to the camp," the woman said coldly, and Fargo saw Tollner hesitate, uncertain of what he should do and unwilling to test the woman's resolve.

The Trailsman stepped from the trees, the barrel of the Colt in his hand. Moving on absolutely noiseless steps, he headed for the woman with the gun. Tollner had to see him, he knew, and he pointed to the second woman and clapped one hand over his mouth. He was at the woman with the pistol in two more strides and he brought the butt of the Colt down on her head just as Tollner dived onto the second woman, clapped a hand over her mouth, and smashed her into unconsciousness with a fast blow.

"We tie them?" Tollner said.

"No time and no need to. We'll be on our way before they come around," Fargo said.

Another of the men was approaching along the edge of the trees with a third following a dozen yards behind. Jennifer got to her feet, straightened her clothes, and met Fargo's glance.

"Be right back," Fargo said. He strode into the trees where he'd left Asa, picked her up, untied her wrists and ankles, pulled the brown sleeveless shift out, and dropped it over her head. He pulled her hand down as she tried to tear at the gag, and yanked her with him, letting her stumble and pulling her to her feet. He saw Jennifer's eyes widen with instant protest as he appeared dragging Asa along.

"You're not bringing her," Jennifer said.

"She's our ticket through the damn bog. She knows the way," Fargo said, and Asa shot fire at him from her black and burning eyes. Tollner's four men had arrived, he saw, and he gestured to Jennifer. "You lead my horse and the filly," he said.

"What about our horses?" Tollner asked.

"I couldn't risk having you bring them to meet me. You'd have been heard. You'll get new horses when we're out of here," Fargo said, and the men grudgingly accepted the truth of his words. He started forward through the trees, Jennifer leading the horses behind him, Tollner and the others bringing up the rear.

Fargo cast a glance at a patch of sky that became visible, and the distant edge bore a faint line of grayness. Dawn wasn't far away. He hurried forward, pulling Asa beside him, to halt when he reached the edge of the giant bog just as the first pink grayness of the new day arrived.

He took the lariat from Jennifer's horse and tied a loop around his waist, knotted it, and tossed it to Jennifer. "Leave six feet of rope between us and tie it around yourself," he said.

"You'll do the same, Tollner, and all the rest of you."

"We'll all be connected. If one goes down, he'll take someone with him, maybe everybody," Tollner said as he finished tying the rope around himself.

"Only it's the other way around, Connected, we might be able to help one another. Alone, there's little chance of that, and if it doesn't work, we can cut ourselves loose," Fargo said. He moved forward, as far as he dared along the one passage he knew held firm ground, and when he halted, he pulled the gag from Asa's mouth. She coughed for a moment, rubbed her lips, and looked at him with hate in her black eyes. "You're far enough from camp now to yell all you want," he said. "I figure they'll be coming to look for us in another hour or two, anyway, soon as they find out what's happened." He pointed out at the vast uncharted terrain of twisted trees and gnarled branches. "Start," he growled at Asa. "You're taking us through."

Her lips curled at him. "Never. I'm taking you no place," she said.

"You took Frank Tupper through, you told me," Fargo said.

"Yes, he tricked me. He said he'd return with me," she said. "But you are worse. He never joined me. You did and you betray me now."

"You did the tricking, honey, and you know it," Fargo growled. "Start leading the way."

"No. You brought me here, but you can't make me take you through," she said scornfully.

Fargo's eyes went to the terrain directly behind where they waited. Jennifer had nearly been sucked to her death there and he took Asa by the shoulders and made her face the terrain. "That's bog. I know that. So do you. Now you take us around it, past it or through it," he ordered.

Asa laughed, a bitter sound. "No, and you can't make me," she said. "You know you can't make me take you through."

"You take us through, dammit," Fargo rasped.

"No," she flung back, dropped to the ground, and sat cross-legged, almost lost in the sleeveless brown shift.

"That your last on it?" Fargo asked.

"That's right," she snapped.

"Then we'll go on our own," Fargo said, and her laugh was a sneer of derision. "We won't need you and we'll not leave you to go running back to bring your friends." Fargo reached and scooped her up in his arms.

"What are you doing?" Asa cried out.

"Getting rid of cheating, lying trouble," Fargo said, and flung her from him in a wide arc.

She hit the bog on her back with a flat, sucking thud that cut off her scream. Part of her went under at once, but she was light and her torso stayed on top of the sucking ooze. Asa tried to struggle free, but the bog clung, pulling her deeper the more she struggled.

Fargo turned away from her and spoke to Jennifer. "Stay behind me. We're going this way," he said, and pointed to his right.

"No," he heard Asa scream. "Don't leave me. No."

Fargo paused, looked back at her, and saw she had gone down to her breasts, and in her face he saw wild fear. She flailed her arms wildly, then felt herself start to sink deeper at once and stopped. Her black eyes burned into him. Fargo turned away, motioning to Jennifer to follow and ignoring the horror he saw in her eyes.

"You can't," she whispered.

"The hell I can't," he growled.

"That's a terrible kind of death, Fargo," Jennifer murmured.

"I never heard there was a good kind," he rasped, and she fell silent.

"No, please . . . no." Asa screamed and Fargo halted again. He turned back to her and saw only her shoulders, arms, and head were still above the ooze. "Please," Asa half-sobbed.

He fastened her with a harsh, uncompromising stare. "You going to take us through?" he said, and saw her black eyes stare back at him. "Maybe this is the last chance for us, too, but it sure as hell is that last one for you," he said. "Yes or no?"

"Yes," she said, her voice breaking. "Yes. Just get me out of here."

He took his own lariat and sent it whirling through the air. The loop landed around her shoulders. When she had it under her armpits, he began to pull her to the firm ground. Her small, light form came free quickly, and when he had her on the ground in front of him, he undid the lariat as she gasped in deep breaths. He let her lie gasping until she had her breath back and the dawn swept the sky. Asa lifted her head and looked at him, her eyes narrowed.

"Time's a-wasting," he said, and she pushed to her feet, half of her caked with mud and slime. He motioned for her to go on ahead of him and she did, carefully moving forward in a straight line, then turning to the left, picking her way down a strip of land. Fargo, close behind her, saw the bubbles of ooze come to the surface not twelve inches from where he walked.

Asa paused at one point, glanced at him, and he saw only rage in her black orbs. "Keeping going," he said. "I gave you a second chance. You won't get another from me."

"You're of the devil," Asa muttered, but she turned and moved forward. His eyes followed her every step as she led the way, swept the trees on both sides that seemed to rise from solid ground yet he knew had their roots deep in the bog. He glanced back and saw the others all staying in line, Jennifer gazing out at the twisted tree shapes with fear. A huge black oak rose up directly in front of them, its heavy roots exposed on all sides as though it were a cypress rising out of some bayou swamp.

Asa led the way to it and halted when she was but a half-dozen feet from the tree. "We'll be going 'around it, close in to the edge of the roots," she said.

"Single-file and stay close together. Let the horses follow last on their own," Fargo ordered.

Tollner and his men moved up behind Jennifer as she let go of the Ovaro's reins, and Fargo waited for her to edge close to him. Asa looked back, waiting, and Fargo nodded at her to go on. She began to move around the base of the huge tree, staying near the exposed roots, he saw, leaning on them with one hand as she moved. He glanced back and saw the Ovaro hadn't followed, the gray filly behind him, and he felt the stab of apprehension go through him.

"What is it?" Jennifer asked, catching the fleeting expression in his face.

"Maybe nothing," he said. "And maybe something." He looked forward at Asa. She moved quickly, lightly, leaning against the roots with one hand, and she danced out of sight for a moment as she rounded the back of the tree. "Slow down," Fargo called out.

"Just keep going," Asa's voice called back. "I'm here waiting for you." Fargo moved forward and heard her footsteps half-race onward and he rounded the tree to find she was out of sight. "Just keep going around," Asa called. "I'm here."

"Come back here where I can see you," Fargo ordered, testing the ground in front of him before he took another step. His foot sank into slime and he pulled it back. "Goddamn," he swore. "Bog. We can't go on."

"She went on," Jennifer said, and Fargo grimaced. "Along the top of the roots," Jennifer breathed.

"Bully's-eye," Fargo said. "She's small and cat-like enough to do it."

106

"Then we'll have to be catlike enough to do it," Jennifer said.

"Calling a duck a swan doesn't make it so."

"Is there any other choice?"

"We stay in place, turn around, and go back," Fargo said. "This explains why the Ovaro didn't follow."

"How?" Jennifer frowned.

"Horse sense," he said. "That's another term for animal instinct. He sensed danger."

"I say we go ahead on the roots. There has to be a trail on the far side of this tree. That's where she's gone," Jennifer said.

"It seems that way," Fargo said, "but I wouldn't be sure of anything about her." He had just uttered the last word when the cry split the forest stillness, and almost instantly after it, there was a yank on the rope tied around his waist.

"Jesus. No, oh, Christ," one of Tollner's men screamed.

Fargo straightened, peered back, and saw two of the men go into the bog. Asa, her hands still upraised, had come around the other side of the tree and barreled into the last man. He plunged from the firm ground, took the second man with him, and the next man followed as the rope holding them together grew taut. Fargo saw Tollner go into the ooze, made a grab for Jennifer as she was yanked sideways by Tollner's falling body, and her hand slid from his grasp. The Trailsman tried to brace himself but he was off balance, and as Jennifer fell, he came after her. He managed to turn and landed in the bog feet-first.

"I'm sinking. Christ, it's pulling me under," Tollner yelled.

"Stay quiet. The more you move, the worse it

gets," Fargo called out, and his eyes found Asa as she looked at him from the firm ground.

"You'll pay now, all of you," she called out, spun on her heel, and ran. Her scream of triumph echoed through the twisted trees and silent bog as she disappeared from sight. But she'd be returning, Fargo knew, with Josiah and the others, to finish whatever the bog failed to do.

Fighting through the ooze, Fargo drew his arm up with the lariat, lifted his hand high, and even as the ooze sucked at him, he sent the lariat circling through the air and caught the loop around a low, thick branch of the big oak. He pulled the loop tight, took a twist of the lariat around his hand, and glanced back at the others. Tollner had sunk down the most but he still had his arms and shoulders above the slime.

"Grab the ropes that connect you together. Each time I say three, you pull, hear me?" Fargo shouted, and received a murmur of response. "One—two—*three*," he began, and at the last number he pulled hard on the rope attached to the tree. He felt the surge as the others pulled with him. "One—two—*three*," he counted again, and kept up the cadenced measure. As they all pulled together, it helped take the weight from his arms and little by little they surged forward with each count. But the clinging, grasping ooze continued to clutch and pull, unwilling to be denied. The tree was so close, yet it seemed so far away, and he heard Jennifer's gasp.

"My arms, I can't go on," she said.

"You'll go on," he threw back savagely. "Pull, dammit." He counted again and felt her pull with him. Suddenly he felt the pull of the bog grow less and the big oak was only inches away. He pulled himself forward the last short distance and felt the touch of firm ground, fought forward again, and dragged himself onto the narrow path of firmness near the tree. He turned, wrapped the lariat around his shoulders, and began to pull Jennifer up. She came, the ooze falling away with a sucking noise, and fell onto the ground beside him.

"Turn around and start pulling. You can rest later," he said harshly, and she turned herself and grasped the rope with him. Abe Tollner was next to pull free of the ooze, and the others came quickly as they helped one another with every pull of their connecting ropes. Finally they all lay on the narrow path and gasped in deep breaths of air.

"We've got to go on," Fargo said. "They'll be coming soon enough."

"We could stay right here and pick them off as they come," Tollner said.

"None of our guns will fire until we clean the ooze and slime out of them," Fargo said. "And there's no way to do that here. We've got to go on, get to someplace where we can make a stand."

"Go on? How, for God's sake?" Jennifer exploded, fear and despair curled in her voice. "Look out there. How do we know where to step, where to turn? We can't go on. All we'll do is go down again, this time for good."

She started to say more but Fargo's hand dug into her shoulder and he shook her hard enough for her brown hair to bounce. "That's enough," he rasped, and she fell silent.

"I've got to agree with her, Fargo," Tollner said dejectedly. "I'd say we try to go back and hightail it the way we came."

"Not enough time. We'll run smack into them," Fargo said. "We're going on through." He saw Jennifer's eyes turn on him with incomprehension. "I didn't just follow little Asa. I watched, studied how she moved and when she turned, and I took in the land on my own," Fargo said. "See those flowers over there?"

"The tall, thin deep-red ones?" Jennifer queried.

"That's right. Cardinal flowers. They grow near brooks and at the edges of swamps. Does that tell you anything?" Fargo asked, and Jennifer's frown held only confusion. "At the *edges* of swamps and near brooks and newly flooded fields. Not *in* swamps, not *in* bogs, the way some flowers do, but at the edges. They insist on moist but firm ground. Every turn she took there were cardinal flowers," he said, and felt the excitement catching in his voice at the telling. "They'll mark the way for us," he said. "Let's move."

Fargo returned to where the Ovaro remained waiting, took the horse's reins, and started to lead the others forward. He moved carefully even as he followed the trail of the deep-red, tall, thin stems. He turned where the flowers rose up to his left, followed again, and the ground continued to stay softly firm. A row of the flowers suddenly branched to the right, blossoming under the low boughs of a sandbar willow. He followed them again and half-smiled as the ground remained firm.

A long, twisting passage of the flowers suddenly turned left, straightened, and ended in a wide field of the red blossoms. "We're through," Fargo shouted. "Damn, we're through." He hurried forward and felt the solid ground underfoot, halted, and waited for the others to come up.

Jennifer came to him, put her hands against his chest. "You're a very special person, Fargo," she murmured.

"That's grateful talk," he muttered.

"Yes, but it's still true," she said, and stepped back. He half-turned his head to one side as he caught the sound of running water.

"This way," he said as he swung onto the Ovaro. He rode on ahead of the others, through a thicket of shadbush, and halted beside the swiftly running, wide stream that cascaded down from the slopes in the distance. A line of dense high shrub ran along near one side of the stream and bright, warm sun bathed the land.

Jennifer, on the gray filly, was first to reach him. She slid from the horse and said, "Oh, God, a chance to get this slime off."

"Later," Fargo said as the others came up. "We clean and dry our guns first, then go back and wait for them. They'll be along pretty damn soon. We had to go very slow and carefully. Asa won't be doing that." He dropped to his knees beside the brook, flipped the shells from the Colt, and immersed the gun in the cool, clear water. Tollner and the others did the same, and when he had the six-gun cleaned, he used a towel from his saddlebag to dry it off, handing the towel to Tollner when he finished and reloaded. He took the big Sharps from its rifle case alongside the saddle and handed it to Jennifer. "You use this," he said.

"I'm not much of a shot," she said.

"Do your best," he answered, and Tollner and the others fell in step beside him as he started back.

"You think all of them will be coming?" Tollner asked.

"Hell, no," Fargo said. "And we only have to bring down some of the men. They'll turn and run then."

"Just like that?" Tollner frowned.

"Just like that," Fargo repeated. "You wait and see."

When they neared the place where they had emerged from the bog, he motioned for everyone to spread out. "Form a half-circle, at least a dozen feet between everybody," he ordered. "Lie flat. Fire from your bellies and stay down." He watched the others sink onto the ground, half-hidden by tall grass, and position themselves. He lay down a dozen feet away from Jennifer and saw the tension in her mud-smeared face, her streak of light-brown hair still somehow untouched. "Don't think. Just shoot," he called to her, and she glanced back and nodded. His eyes returned to the treeline of the bog and he put his face down on the earth, waited and felt his lips draw back. They were coming and not all on foot. He heard the vibration of horse's hooves and raised his head. "Take those on horseback first," he called.

"Got it," Tollner answered.

Fargo drew the big Colt, stretched his arm forward, and his eyes were on the trees as the figures burst forth. Three horses, Bartholomew on one, two men he didn't know on the other two. The others followed on foot and he saw Asa, in her buckskin outfit, three men behind her, then three women with rifles and then another line of both men and women. The Trailsmen took aim at Bartholomew, fired, and the man bucked in the saddle, fell forward across the saddle horn, and toppled from the horse as if in slow motion.

Tollner and the rest of his men opened fire and Fargo saw the other two horsemen go down. The others on foot dived to the ground for protection, but Fargo caught one man in his sights, fired again, and the man showered blood and bone into the air even before he hit the ground.

Tollner and his men were firing furiously now, some of their shots wild, but Fargo saw one of the women half-rise, her blouse stained with red, and topple sideways to lay still. It was then that he heard Josiah's voice from the trees out of range.

"Leave them. Come back. Leave them be," Josiah shouted. "The devil has his victories."

Fargo saw the grass move as the followers crawled back by the trees. "Hold fire," he called out, and waited as those who had come to attack crawled away, staying on their bellies until they reached the trees. They rose then and ran into the dimness, and he thought he glimpsed Asa's small, darting form but he couldn't be sure. He pushed to his feet and saw Jennifer rise and hand the Sharps to him.

"I don't know if I hit anybody," she said. "I don't want to know."

"They hightailed it, just as you said they would, Fargo," Abe Tollner admitted. "How'd you know?"

"Building the community is first above all else with them. They can't afford to lose men. They need all those womenfolk making babies," Fargo said. "Now let's get cleaned up." He turned, led the Ovaro back to where the stream ran down the slope, and halted as Jennifer came up to him. "Ladies first," he said.

"Not with an audience," she said, and he shrugged.

"You really hang on to modesty, I'll give you that," he said.

"And you keep trying," she snapped.

He laughed and moved to the other side of the dense thicket of shadbush as she began to pull off clothes. Tollner and his men waited beside him until Jennifer reappeared in a fresh shirt and Levi's and carrying her cleaned and wet clothes in one hand.

Fargo let Tollner and the others go first and Jennifer sat down beside him, gray eyes studying him.

"What happens now, Fargo?" she asked.

"We go on, come morning, to the foot of Kings

Peak," he said. "That's where Tupper was headed. Seems he has two brothers there."

"I could stand a little time to get over this. I think everyone could," Jennifer said.

"I've lost too much time already," Fargo said gruffly, rising as Tollner and the men returned, and strode through the brush to the stream. He took a change of clothes and a towel from his saddlebag, washed the slime and ooze from himself and his clothes, and when he finished, the sun still hung in the afternoon sky. "We ride till it's time to bed down," he said.

"You ride," Tollner reminded him. "And the girl."

"You can follow our prints. I'll find a spot to bed down," Fargo said, and turned the Ovaro southeast. With Jennifer riding a few paces behind, he skirted the foothills of the main mass of the Uinta Mountains. As dusk settled, he found a spot to camp, halted, built a small fire, and was warming strips of beef jerky when Tollner and the others came up. They ate hungrily, weariness in their faces, and quickly found themselves places to sleep. The small fire burned out and Jennifer lay down near him with her cape. He undressed to his underdrawers and felt her eyes watching him.

"I wish I could understand you, Fargo," Jennifer said.

"Does it matter?"

"Maybe I'd like to know what you're all about inside."

"I do what has to be done."

"Yes, I keep forgetting," she said, and a wry smile touched her lips. He turned and reached out, closed one arm behind her head, and drew her to him.

She clutched at the cape immediately as it started

to fall away. "What are you doing?" She frowned, but his mouth closed over hers, held, pressed.

He felt the softness of her lips before she drew her mouth tight and he pulled back. "Just to let you know," he said.

"Let me know what?" Jennifer asked.

"That you don't have to let one thing get in the way of another." He laughed and fell back onto his bedroll. "Kind of a lesson in being honest."

"Did you learn a lesson about being too eager?" she snapped, turning her back to him and submerging herself under the cape.

He smiled and closed his eyes. He felt a twinge of sympathy for Jennifer. The hard part was still ahead for her. Maybe for him, too, he grunted as he fell asleep.

6

The morning came in bright and warm and Fargo found a cluster of mulberry bushes nearby that served as breakfast.

Tollner came to him and the three men formed a half-circle behind him. "We need horses. Eddie says he knows a rancher north of here. Maybe two days' walking but we can get horses there," the man said.

"I can't wait for you," Fargo said. "Time's too important."

"We're not asking you to wait for us," Tollner said. "We're backing off. You didn't want us along in the first place. We figure you saved our necks and we owe you."

"Fair enough," Fargo said, a little surprised. "What about Eason and the others? They probably still owe you money."

"We got most of it up front," Tollner said. "But there's something else you ought to know. They're afraid of this Frank Tupper."

"Afraid of him?" Fargo frowned.

"That's right. They want him back but not because he robbed their damn bank. They're afraid of him. I don't know why, but they are," Tollner said.

"How do you know that?"

"I heard them talking. Besides, we had orders to be sure and kill Tupper if we couldn't get him back," Tollner said. "That's more than just wanting a bank robber brought in."

Fargo's lips pursued as he digested Tollner's words. "Much obliged," he said.

"Good luck," the man replied. He nodded to Jennifer and turned away. The other three men swung in beside him and began to stride northward.

Fargo waited till they'd grown small in the distance before he climbed onto the pinto again and turned the horse toward the foothills of the mountains. He shifted course after a few thousand yards to ride alongside the foothills.

Jennifer came up beside him and he saw her lovely, aquiline face was tight. "Tollner was talking about Eason and Sheriff Sideman," she said.

"He didn't say that," Fargo answered evenly.

"He didn't say it, but that's what he meant," she insisted. "I know Daddy isn't involved in anything wrong."

"He's thick as mud with Eason and Sideman. You know that, girl," Fargo said quietly.

"He's the town judge. He works closely with the sheriff and the mayor. That doesn't mean he's involved with them in anything wrong," Jennifer returned stubbornly.

"I know it's hard," Fargo said softly, but she glared back.

"What's hard?" she snapped.

"When your heart tells you one thing and your head another," he said not ungently.

"Go to hell," she flung at him. She slapped the gray on the rump and sent the horse into a gallop.

He let her race on and watched her disappear over the top of the next slope, but he kept the Ovaro at a slow, steady trot. He glimpsed her still riding hard when he crested the slope and started down, but finally she slowed and halted at a brook where she waited for him to ride up. She returned to the saddle and rode beside him, anger in her silence. And something more, he knew, a fear she refused to face . . .

He rode through the morning, halting to let the horses rest a little past noon. Jennifer continued her silence. She could be stubborn, he saw, and he made no move to coax her out of her anger as they rode on.

It was midafternoon when he reined up, leaned from the saddle, and scooped a wrist gauntlet from the ground. He studied the rubbed hide. It had a symmetrical design not unlike forest leaves painted onto the hide. "Ute," he grunted, and his eyes went back to the ground where he took in the unshod hoofprints that crossed their path. "They were galloping. Four of them," he read aloud, and pointed to another set of prints dug deep into the soil—narrow, rounded points at the front, the hind and front prints virtually identical. "Chasing an elk," Fargo said, but turned the pinto toward the mountains. "We'll move right just to play safe."

He led the way a little closer to the foothills. Toward the end of the day he halted again, the terrain now made up of thick, tangled brush and almost impenetrable thickets. In a relatively clear area they dismounted and tethered the horses at one side. He quickly gathered enough wood for a small fire before night descended, and he warmed the strips of beef from his saddlebag as Jennifer settled down across from him.

She flashed a glance of exasperation across the low fire. "Do you ever have any faith in anyone?" she tossed at him. "Do you ever believe in anybody?"

"It's happened," he answered.

"What does it take to make it happen?" she

sneered angrily. "Lightning bolts? A voice from above?"

"A voice from inside," he said quietly.

Her lips tightened as she turned away from his calm, steady stare. He could feel the anger churning inside her. He had just finished the last of his beef strip when his nostrils flared. He took another deep draft of the warm night air and his eyes narrowed.

"Pigs," he murmured.

"What?" Jennifer asked, frowning at him.

"Pigs, not far away," Fargo said.

"Pigs?" Jennifer echoed. "You mean wild pigs, javelinas?"

"No, javelinas wouldn't be this far north," he said. The very dangerous peccaries the natives called javelinas were mostly found in Arizona, south Texas, New Mexico, and south of the border, he knew. "These are wild pigs," he told her. "The domestic kind gone wild."

She drew her breath in deeply. "Yes, I catch the scent now," she said.

"Settlers often lose a half-dozen pigs, especially when traveling. The pigs run off, mate, live on all the natural food around here—roots and tubers and fruits and berries—and become a pack."

"Then they're not fierce like the javelinas," Jennifer said.

"Not like the javelinas with those long tusk teeth and rotten tempers," Fargo said. "But they can be dangerous. They can bite and those sharp hooves can cut a man to pieces. They won't come attacking like the javelinas, but if they're disturbed or feel threatened, a pack of them can be plenty dangerous." He stared into the darkness but he could see nothing. However, the smell of them had grown stronger, pungent and unmistakable. "They probably caught scent of the beef strips warming," he said, rising to his feet.

"What are you going to do?" Jennifer asked as he strode to the Ovaro.

"Explore some, see if I can find where they are. They'll hear and smell me nosing around and maybe they'll go on their way then," he said. He drew the big Sharps from its saddlecase. There'd not be enough light to shoot but he could use it as a club if he had to. "Meanwhile, you stay here by the fire. Undress and get ready to bed down. I won't be far."

He moved away from the dim glow of the fire and stepped into the blackness beyond. Using his nose as a guide, he started to move through the thick brush. He moved slowly, carefully. He wanted them to become aware of his presence without setting them off in fright or defensive anger. Holding the rifle by the barrel, he paused, hearing a half-dozen low grunts and the sound of their thick, low bodies shuffling through the brush. They had moved ahead of him. He pressed forward again. He peered through the blackness and saw a spot where the moonlight managed to sift down and he managed to glimpse three of the animals scurry into the brush. But there were more than three, the sound of them indicating at least a dozen.

He moved carefully forward once more and breathed deeply. They still continued to move ahead of him, but shuffling their way, no alarm in their movements. He halted to wait and listen, satisfied he'd been successful, when the night suddenly exploded in sound, the scream Jennifer's voice followed by the cacophony of loud, angry snorts and grunts.

"Shit," Fargo swore. He raced forward as he heard Jennifer scream again, the sound of her falling before the scream ended. The thud of small, sharp hooves racing back and forth, and now Jenni-fer's voice in gasped cries of pain.

Fargo crashed through the dense brush, the scur-rying, darting thick bodies coming into view. He brought the rifle down across the fat backs that crossed in front of him. The blows brought only grunted snorts that were more annoyance than pain. He caught another gasped groan of pain from Jen-nifer as he charged forward. He used the rifle stock almost as if it were a giant broom, clubbing back and forth with it. As the hogs scurried away, he glimpsed Jennifer, facedown on the ground. He ran toward her, half-turned as he heard the hard clop of sharp hooves coming at him from the side, and saw a big, angry hog charging at him.

He leapt backward, swung the rifle in his hands, and fired directly at the fat snout and red-angry little eyes. The hog's head exploded in globs of red-stained fat and the sound of the shot sent the others grunting and snorting into the blackness.

Fargo knelt down beside Jennifer and saw the bleeding cuts on her back and arms where the sharp hooves had run over her. He lifted her unconscious form as he cursed into the blackness. She'd come out here and run right into the herd in the darkness.

"Why, dammit?" he asked her unconscious form. "Why in hell did you come out here?" Still mutter-ing under his breath, he put her down beside the dying fire, took the blanket, and spread it out and placed her on it before returning to his saddlebag and finding the small cork-stopped vial.

He put the vial down on the blanket and began to take her clothes off, her blouse first, then the che-mise beneath it, and last the skirt which he unbut-toned and slipped down her legs. He used her blouse to wipe the blood from her wounds and quickly applied the salve from the vial, rubbing it over each

121

cut and atop each bruise mark. When he finished he sat back and had time to take in the long loveliness of her smoothly rounded shoulders and longish breasts, which nonetheless curved beautifully into deep cups, each centered by a faintly pink nipple on an equally faint pink circle. She had a long torso, ribs barely covered, and a flat belly that ended in a modest V of tightly curled thickness. Long, lean, yet nicely curved thighs and long calves formed smooth legs that were graceful even in absolute stillness. He rose, went to her horse, and returned with the cape and spread it over her just as she moaned. She stirred and he watched her eyes come open slowly, flicker, pull awake again, and finally focus on him.

"You're cut and bruised pretty good," he told her. "But you're lucky. It could've been a lot worse."

Jennifer closed her eyes for a long moment and pulled them open again. "I hurt," she breathed.

"You will, till the salve I put on starts to work. That'll take a couple of hours," Fargo said.

"Salve?" She frowned.

"Birch-bark compress, comfrey, hyssop, and wintergreen," Fargo said. "It can work wonders."

Jennifer stared at him for a moment as the tiny furrow gathered on her smooth brow. She lifted the cape and looked down at her self and he heard her short gasp of shock and embarrassment. He shrugged as she brought her eyes back to him.

"I kept my eyes closed," he offered. She tossed him a glance of total disbelief. "What the hell were you doing out there?" he rasped, anger spiraling instantly with the question. "I told you to stay by the fire."

"I started to undress and then I realized you could see me by the fire," she said.

"I wasn't looking, dammit," he growled.

"But you might've been," she said. "So I decided to change away from the fire. I went into the brush and suddenly they were knocking into me. I remember going down and the first one that stepped on me. God, it hurt."

"Damn high price for modesty," Fargo remarked.

"Yes," she conceded ruefully. "Especially when it all went for nothing." She lay back with a deep, groaning sigh.

"Go to sleep," he said. "As I said, you got away lucky."

The fire flickered out altogether as he undressed and stretched out on his bedroll. He listened to the silence of the deep, tangled forest, a silence that was alive with the sounds of soft wings, murmured buzzings and hummings, and scurrying paws. He had just closed his eyes when he heard Jennifer's murmur, almost a whisper.

"Did you like what you saw?" she said, and he heard no edge in her voice, only a little-girl plaintiveness.

"Indeed," he said.

"Good night," she murmured, and he smiled as he closed his eyes and fell asleep in moments.

The warm morning sun woke him and he rose, washed, and let Jennifer continue to sleep. He wandered, found a tree of sweet wild pears, and brought a half-dozen back to find Jennifer sitting up. "How do you feel?" he asked.

"Almost great. That salve really works," she said.

"I think I ought to take a look. You might need a little more," he said, and expected a protest.

Instead, she turned onto her stomach and stretched out for him. He drew the cape back and examined the cuts and bruises on her back and legs, where most of the damage had been done. They had healed even faster than he'd expected, and he applied a little more salve in two places and took a moment to enjoy the long, lean curve of her body, her narrow hips, and a tight rear that rose smoothly to go down into her long, lithe legs.

He rose to his feet and walked to the Ovaro. "Think you can ride?" he asked as he put the salve jar back into his saddlebag.

"Oh, sure," she said as she pulled clothes on and he let the horses go loose to graze on a broad swath of bluegrass. When they'd eaten their fill and Jennifer had finished the pears, he moved on, still skirting the foothills, and watched closely as Jennifer's endurance faded quickly. He stopped frequently and let her rest, seeing the gratitude in her eyes.

By late afternoon they came to a deep, wide stream that was literally filled with fish. Using a sharpened length of branch, he effortlessly speared a rainbow trout. He flipped its speckled beauty on the grass, and with the sharp, double-edged throwing knife in his calf holster, he did a better-than-average job of boning the fish.

Jennifer made a small fire and Fargo fashioned a skillet out of a long flat stone he found near the stream. Dinner was cooking by the time darkness came to blanket the land. Moonlight shone down on the cleared space beside the stream, and when they had finished eating, Fargo brought out his bedroll and stretched out on it.

"Feeling better?" he asked as Jennifer came to sit on the edge of the bedroll beside him.

"Very much better," she said. She leaned back on her elbows and he watched the concave curve of her breasts under the blouse.

"We'll reach Kings Peak, come morning," he said. "And maybe Frank Tupper, if that's where he's holed up."

"Then you start back with him," Jennifer said.

"Soon as I get my hands on him," Fargo said. Jennifer folded her arms around her knees and watched the moonlight sparkle on the stream. The night stayed warm and Fargo began to pull off clothes. "Better get some sleep. No telling what tomorrow may bring," he said.

"I'm not tired," she said. "I guess the meal revived me." She turned and her eyes moved over his almost nude form as he stretched out on the bedroll. He felt the tiny furrow of surprise slide across his brow as Jennifer turned to face him and began to unbutton her blouse, slowly pulled the garment off, undid her skirt, rose to her knees, and let it slide to the ground. He let his eyes enjoy the long, lean loveliness of her, breasts swaying ever so faintly above the long torso, the tightly curled nap its own black triangle of provocativeness.

"What happened to modesty?" Fargo asked quietly.

"Seems pointless now, after last night," Jennifer said. She came forward and her arms rose, slid around his neck, and he watched the longish breasts lift and the light-pink tips were already standing firm. Her lips came onto his, sweet wanting, pressed harder, softly firm, hesitant yet bold. He let her lips stay on his but returned only a timid response. His hand came up, pressed against her back for a moment, and drew away.

Jennifer pulled back and frowned at him. "What is it?" she asked.

"I was warned about being too eager," he said blandly.

"Damn you," Jennifer murmured, and her mouth fell over his again, harsher this time, her tongue coming out, touching, drawing back, and coming out again.

He swallowed his laugh as his arms came up,

wrapped around her, and rolled her onto the bedroll. He heard her gasp of pleasure as he cupped one hand around her breast, let his thumb move back and forth across the light-pink tip.

"Aaah . . . aaaah . . . so good, so nice," Jennifer murmured. When he brought his lips down to the soft-firm tip, she uttered quivering little gasps. He circled her breast with his tongue, tracing a path around the edge of the light-pink areola. Jennifer cried out in pleasure as he pulled on the pink nipple with a gentle harshness.

Her hands clutched at the back of his neck and she pulled his face down over her breasts, pressed him hard against her. He sucked on one, then the other, and Jennifer's cries rose, delight curled in each quivering sigh. He let his hand trace a slow trail down her long torso, pausing at the tiny indentation in the center of her flat belly, circling ever so slowly. He felt her quiver. His hand moved down, came to the dense tight curls, pressed, and felt the hardened roundness of her pubic mound.

"Oh, God, oh, oh . . . aaaah, oh, nice, so nice, so nice," Jennifer murmured, words floating from her on long moaning sighs of pleasure. He saw her long, lean legs fall from side to side together, invitation and refusal in one, and he brought his hand lower, through the tight curls.

"No, oh, no . . . oh, oh, God," Jennifer called out, and in her voice was a dichotomy of the emotions: ecstasy and fear, wanting and uncertainty. He held his fingers curled into a fist, stayed motionless, and Jennifer's hips lifted and fell back and her legs, still held tightly together, continued to fall from side to side. Tiny whimpering sounds came from her while her own hands dug into his back. He moved his balled hand a fraction, pressed down between her thighs, and her cries rose at once. He felt her hands flatten, begin to push against him. But he pressed down further, only a fraction deeper but enough to rest his fingers against the dark portal and feel the moistness of her. His hand uncurled, touching the very edges of the slippery lips.

Jennifer almost leapt under him, her hips lifting, long legs falling apart this time. He touched again, deeper, and she gave long, trailing cry. He swung his body over her and pressed his throbbing organ into her thighs.

"Oh, God, God, oh, no . . . no, oh, oh," Jennifer cried out even as her legs stayed open to find their way against his hips. He slid forward, into the wetness of her, and immediately the tight contractions clutched at him. He slowed, but her hands pulled against him.

"Go on, go on, oh, yes, yes . . . oh, God, yes," she breathed, and he came forward again and felt her body shudder under him. She moved with him, long legs sliding back and forth against his hips, her long torso drawing in and out with her every slow thrust. Jennifer's hands pulled his face down to the longish breasts as she moved with him, her body pushing itself back and forth with his rhythm, all of her consumed with the total pleasure of the flesh.

He felt himself filling her completely as she gasped and cried out, quivered and groaned, until the very night trembled with the sound of her. Her hands suddenly came up, almost smashing against the sides of his face, and he stared down at her and saw the gray eyes growing wild, almost smoking with a gray fire and something else close to panic.

"I'm . . . I'm coming . . . oh, my God, Oh, Fargo, I'm coming . . . now, now, now," Jennifer screamed, her voice spiraling, and he felt the contractions tighten around him, her long legs straightening out to dig thighs against him as a scissor of flesh.

As her spiraling scream finally faded away and her long body continued to quiver, her thighs dropped down from against him and Jennifer fell back, her gray eyes growing soft as she pulled him down to her, smothered her body with his.

"Guess I learned one of those two answers." He smiled.

"I'm practically a virgin. It was long ago and nothing really happened," Jennifer said.

"You were," Fargo said and she smiled again.

"I lay corrected," she said, snuggled herself against him. "I'm suddenly very sleepy," she murmured, and her eyes were closed, her lips parted in sleep before he had a chance to reply.

He kept his arms around her as he let himself sleep, and the warm night was all the blanket they needed.

He slept soundly and the morning sun slowly slid over his body when the new day dawned. But it was not the touch of the sun that woke him as he felt Jennifer's hand close around his groin, find him, and begin to caress and stroke. He pulled his eyes open even as he felt himself responding to her touch, and he saw the intense frown of pleasure on her face as she watched him grow under her caresses. "You take to the habit quickly," he said.

Jennifer's head drew up to meet his eyes, but her hand stayed around him. "I didn't think there'd be much chance with Frank Tupper in town," she said.

"Probably not," he said, and her lips reached up for his. Her long legs came up, swung over him, and he felt her hand guide him to her and draw back only when he slowly slid into the already lubricious sanctuary of pleasure.

"Uuuuuuh," Jennifer murmured. Her long torso began to draw back and forth at once, drawing him in deeply, the flesh savoring the flesh, and her

mouth came down over his, her tongue thrusting
into him in rhythm with every long stroke of her
body. When the time came for that final burst of
ecstasy, she swung onto her back with him still
inside her and exploded in a long, wailing cry that
only trailed away when her shuddering body grew
still. "Oh, God," Jennifer murmured, and clung to
him. "I don't want to leave here." She gasped in
protest when he drew from her and sat back on his
knees.

'Get yourself together, honey," he said gently.
"Time's moving on."

She sighed reluctantly and rose and he sat back
and enjoyed watching her as she stepped into the
stream and washed, her long-torsoed figure glisten-
ing under the morning sun, her longish breasts
swaying beautifully with her every movement until
finally she emerged and used the towel to dry herself.

He washed and dressed quickly and rode south
while the morning sun was still high in an almost
cloudless sky.

The Uinta Mountains rose up at his right beyond
the foothills and he kept a steady pace until he
caught sight of the green-gray mass of earth that
rose up to tower over the others. "Kings Peak," he
breathed, and sent the Ovaro toward the land that
spread out at the base of the mountain. He slowed
when he neared the land that rolled down from the
mountain like so many earthbound waves, and he
finally glimpsed the thin line of smoke that rose up
beyond a thicket of mountain ash.

Fargo moved closer, stayed inside the tree cover,
and glanced at Jennifer. A mixture of apprehension
and tension colored her face, but he continued to
go forward until the house came into sight, low, a
slanted roof with a chimney, a front yard littered
with extra wagon wheels, small animal traps, and

wood crates. He saw a high fence with hooks on it to hang pelts and he swung down from the Ovaro. "If these are his brothers they're small-time trappers, it seems," Fargo said.

"Why don't we just ride up?" Jennifer suggested. "He doesn't know anyone's chasing him."

"He knows, unless he's a complete fool," Fargo answered.

"He wouldn't expect it to be a man and a woman riding up together," she said.

Fargo smiled. "You stay here," he said, drawing a frown from her.

"I don't mind helping," she said with a touch of hurt in her voice.

"You'll help by staying here," he said, and led the Ovaro through the trees to where he could see the rear of the house. A low-roofed shed, open at one side, held three horses and two mules. Two of the horses were ordinary saddle mounts, the third a heavyset, deep-chested gray, with a wide, flat back and thick legs. Fargo's eyes narrowed as he climbed onto the Ovaro. Sometimes the only way to catch a rabbit was to flush him out. He sent the Ovaro nosing out of the trees and toward the house. A man in tattered Levi's and a gray undershirt stepped out of the house, a dry, scraggly beard covering most of his face, a rifle held casually in one hand. Fargo saw his face screw into an inquiring grimace and his eyes carefully size him up.

"How do," Fargo said pleasantly, but his eyes were on the doorway of the house as the second figure appeared, the same height as the first man but without the beard and bare-chested over baggy trousers. Both men had small, peering eyes with a perpetual squint, Fargo noted.

"'Something we can do for you, mister?" the bearded one asked.

"Maybe," the Trailsman said blandly. "The name's Fargo, Skye Fargo."

"Fred Tupper. This my brother Ned," the man said.

"Been looking all over for a real strong packhorse, and the gray in your shed would sure fill the bill. I'd like to buy him from you," Fargo said.

"You figuring to trap around here?" Fred Tupper asked.

"Not around here. South farther into the Uintas," Fargo said pleasantly. "Looks as if you boys trap."

"That's right," Fred Tupper said, and peered hard at the big man on the Ovaro. "What brings you this way, Fargo?" he questioned.

Fargo paused a moment before answering. He wanted to make them nervous rather than suspicious. "Got some business on the side to do," he said.

The man's squint stayed on his face as he turned the answer in his mind. "The gray's not for sale," he said.

"I'll offer you a real good price for him, more than he's worth, but I just hanker for a horse like that," Fargo answered.

"No sale," Ned Tupper put in firmly, and Fargo decided that though the bearded one looked more imposing, Ned Tupper called the shots.

"Too bad." Fargo swept the house with his eyes. He wanted to press a little harder and he turned a rueful smile on the two men. "Well, if I can't buy the horse, can I buy a cup of coffee?" he asked. "Used up the last I had three days back and my teeth are on edge now. I need a good cup of coffee every day."

He saw the two men exchange glances, hesitate, and it was Ned Tupper again who answered. "Don't like to be inhospitable, friend, but we were just about to go out and we don't have a pot on. It'd take fifteen minutes to brew a fresh pot and we don't have the time."

Fargo shrugged again and smiled pleasantly. "Guess this isn't my day," he said. "I'll be passing this way again in a few days, I expect. Think about the horse. My offer stands."

"A few days?" Fred Tupper echoed.

"More or less," Fargo said. He nodded at the two men and moved the Ovaro forward. He rode on slowly, across the open space and into the trees on the other side of the house, where he halted and peered back to see both men hurry into the house. Staying in the trees, Fargo executed a long, wide circle that brought him around to the other side of the house and the tree cover where he'd left Jennifer.

She studied him as he halted beside her. "I could hear,"she said. "Doesn't seem to me you found out a lot."

"Enough," he said. "His horse is there."

"He could've changed to a fresh horse. That doesn't mean he's there," she countered.

"Those two are down at the heels. They'd have been happy to sell off that big gray if he wasn't needed," Fargo said. "Frank Tupper's in there. That's why they couldn't let me stay around for a cup of coffee."

"You ever think maybe they were on their way out?" Jennifer asked. "People do tell the truth, you know."

"Some people and some times, but not those two and not this time," Fargo rasped as he slid from the Ovaro. "If those two leave in the next ten minutes, I'll eat my hat," he said, and dropped to a crouch as he waited. Jennifer stayed on the horse and he let the ten minutes go by, added another ten before he got to his feet. "They're all inside trying to decide whether I was searching for Frank Tupper or not," he said.

"You know what they'll decide, too?" Jennifer asked tartly.

"They'll decide that Frank can't take the chance I'm not," Fargo said. "He'll be leaving on the gray before day's out."

"What if you're wrong?" Jennifer slid from the horse to lean against a tree. "Suppose he doesn't leave? What do you plan to do then?"

"There's more than one way to flush a rabbit," Fargo said, and settled down to wait. He guessed that hardly an hour had gone by when the two men emerged from the house, each carrying a rifle this time, and they halted and peered in all directions. Ned Tupper waved an arm and Fargo straightened as the third man came out, tall, half-bald, a pinched face of chalk-white skin. Slightly stoop-shouldered. Frank Tupper wore a black vest over a long-sleeved white shirt and black trousers; he looked a lot more like a bookkeeper than a bank robber.

To Fargo's surprise, all three men went around to the rear of the house and reappeared on their horses, Frank Tupper on the big gray, his brothers flanking him. They rode east together and the Trailsman watched from the trees, let them disappear over a hill before he swung onto the Ovaro.

"Tupper is getting some brotherly protection, it seems," Fargo muttered.

"What, now?" Jennifer asked.

"We follow," Fargo said. "I figure the two brothers will turn back after a while."

"Why do you think that?" Jennifer asked, a touch of exasperation in her voice. "Maybe they'll protect him all the way."

"Frank's the only one with a traveling pack and a

saddlebag on his horse," Fargo answered, and drew a wry smile from the young woman.

"You do see with different eyes," she murmured. "Can you see the end of it?"

"The end I see is my way," Fargo said gruffly. He sent the Ovaro forward into a slow trot. He hung back, letting the three men stay out of sight, content to follow their tracks, which turned right and led into the foothills.

The afternoon shadows had begun to lengthen when he saw the hoofprints change character, grow closer together, and he slowed the Ovaro as he followed a narrow pathway along a low slope. He drew the pinto into the thick cover of the trees and Jennifer followed until, a few hundred yards on, he saw the small cabin and the three horses tethered outside. He slid to the ground and motioned for Jennifer to do the same.

"A trapper's line cabin," Fargo murmured. "They figure brother Frank can hole up here for a spell, leastwise till they see if I come back."

He had just ended the sentence when the three men emerged from the cabin and Frank Tupper stayed near the door while his two brothers mounted their steeds. Fargo drew the big Colt from his holster and Jennifer's frown was instant.

"You going to take down the two of them?" she whispered.

"Not unless I have to," he answered. "No sense in pointless killing."

"Then why draw?" she asked.

"They could catch wind of us. I'll be ready if they do," he said, and his eyes stayed on the men as they paused on their horses. The bearded one half-turned his horse and Fargo watched him sniff the air. "He's a trapper. His nose is part of his existence, sensitive to every damn scent in the air," Fargo whispered, his eyes on the man.

Fred Tupper continued to sniff and squint and Fargo cursed silently. The man had caught a scent, probably their horses, Fargo guessed, but the scent wasn't defined enough for him to be certain as he scanned the trees that surrounded the little cabin. Fred Tupper continued to draw deep breaths through his nostrils, but the scent of his own horse got in the way and Fargo drew a sigh of relief as the man began to ride away. Ned Tupper followed, both casting a wave back at their brother, who went back into the cabin.

The last long shadows slid across the small clearing and Fargo listened to the sound of the two horses recede into the distance, but he stayed motionless in the trees and let the night descend.

Lamplight stretched out from the open door of the cabin like a narrow yellow pathway and Fargo crept forward, the Colt in his hand. Jennifer followed him from the trees and he moved quickly across the open space to the outside wall of the cabin. When he reached the doorway, he whirled. Frank Tupper had been stretched out on a bunk, he saw, and the man sat up, astonishment on his face.

"Don't," Fargo said as the man started to reach for a holster hanging at the corner of the bunk, and Frank Tupper froze in motion. "No dumb moves, nobody gets hurt," Fargo said, and Tupper drew his arm back and stared at him.

"Ned and Fred thought you'd gone on," the man said, a wistfulness in his voice.

"I know," Fargo said.

"They send you?" Frank Tupper asked, and Fargo nodded. "I figured they'd send somebody after me," the man said. "Or come themselves." Fargo saw Frank Tupper's eyes go past him as Jennifer stepped into the room and watched the man's jaw drop in surprise. "Miss Hibbs," Tupper breathed.

Fargo met the quick, glance Jennifer threw at him. "That's why I didn't have you ride up to the house with me," he said. "I figured he'd recognize you."

"Why'd you think that?" She frowned.

"He was no bank robber passing through, not the way Eason and the sheriff wanted him. What Abe Tollner said only confirmed that much," Fargo said. "He was involved with them somehow. You knew it, but you kept quiet about it."

"I didn't think it was important," she said quickly.

"Bullshit, honey. You knew I'd figure it tied Daddy in even deeper," Fargo said, and Jennifer's eyes narrowed at him. He caught the faint swish of air as Frank Tupper decided to take advantage of the diversion and dive for his gun. Fargo's shot sent a shower of wood splinters up from the corner of the bunk.

Tupper dropped to the floor. "All right," he cried out.

"I told you, don't do anything stupid," Fargo growled. The man lay still, facedown on the floor as he nodded. "Get my lariat," Fargo threw at Jennifer, and she backed out the doorway and returned quickly with the rope. He holstered his Colt as he bound Tupper hand and foot and tossed the man back onto the bunk. "We'll spend the night here and leave, come morning," he said to Jennifer.

She nodded, went outside, changed into her nightclothes, and returned, the cape around her shoulders, the blanket in her hand. She spread it on the floor while Fargo turned off the lamp, and lay down beside him and he felt her hand on his arm.

"He worked for Mayor Eason," she murmured.

"As an assistant. That's all I know, and I still think it's not important."

"Go to sleep," Fargo growled, and she drew her hand away, turned on her side, and he heard her steady breathing a few minutes after. She was still defending the judge, still holding high the torch of loyalty. It wasn't important anymore. The pain of truth would be hers in time. Or maybe she could manage to avoid seeing the facts. He had Molly and Amy's ticket to freedom in his hands. That's all that mattered now, he vowed as he let sleep draw itself over him.

7

Fargo woke first in the morning and found a small trickle of a stream near the cabin, enough to wash in and refill his canteen. He untied Frank Tupper and let the man freshen up. When Jennifer rose, he took Tupper to the side of the cabin and had the man empty his saddlebag. He appropriated a hunting knife and a box of bullets, put everything into his own saddlebag along with the man's gun.

Jennifer was dressed when he led Tupper back and motioned for him to mount up. The man climbed onto the big gray and Fargo swung in beside him. Tupper glanced at Jennifer as she fell in on the other side of him. "I never expected they'd send you after me, Miss Hibbs," he said.

"They didn't. Fargo brought me along," Jennifer said stiffly.

Frank Tupper's shrug was rueful. "Then I never expected anyone would find me, not after I managed to get through that damn bog," he said.

"Nobody else could have," Jennifer said with a glance at Fargo.

Frank Tupper sent a sideways gaze at the big man riding beside him. "I'm innocent, you know. They set up the bank robbery, shot those two tellers, and blamed me for it," he said.

"Why?" Fargo said as they rode.

"So's they could have a reason to hang me quick

after they realized I'd found out what they've been doing for years," Tupper said.

"You mean Mayor Eason and Sheriff Sideman," Jennifer cut in.

Frank Tupper looked uncomfortable. "They were all in it together, including the judge, miss," he said.

"No, you're wrong there," Jennifer said. "Whatever it was, he wasn't part of it."

Fargo watched Frank Tupper shrug again, the gesture half-helplessness and half-apology. "What did you find out?" he asked.

"All the details of how they've been stealing the town blind for years. The money in the town treasury is all on paper. The real money's in their pockets, siphoned off for years, from the bank, from the money taken from prisoners, from town taxes paid in by the people. They were dumb enough to keep a record of how they divided it for their own use, and I found out, all the fancy switching of funds, the phony deeds from the mayor's office and approved by the judge so it all looked straight," the man said.

"Maybe you made a mistake," Jennifer said. "Maybe you didn't interpret whatever you saw correctly. Did you ever think of that?"

"I thought plenty about it. It was all done cleverly. The truth took a lot of putting together," Tupper said.

"Maybe you just put it together all wrong, at least so far as my father is concerned," Jennifer snapped righteously.

Tupper shrugged again and looked at Fargo. "You take me back there, I'm a dead man. There won't be any trial."

"You got anything more than words?" Fargo queried.

Frank Tupper's face tightened. "If I did, I'm not telling you. Hell, you're working for them," he said. "There's a federal marshal in Vernal. That's where I was heading. Take me to him." Fargo peered at the man's face. "I'm not asking you to let me go. Take me to the marshal. That ought to say something to you," Tupper insisted. "I'll tell him everything."

Fargo turned the man's offer in his mind. Frank Tupper could be just trying to buy time so he could fiind a way to break free. Or he could be telling the truth. Either way, Molly couldn't afford the risk. "You're going back," he said grimly.

"Dammit, mister, what's it take to reach you?" Tupper blurted out angrily.

"More than you have for now," Fargo rasped. "Ride and shut up." He increased the Ovaro's pace, made sure Tupper stayed beside him, and continued to ride hard until the day drew to an end. "We'll camp here," he said as he pulled into a glen of bur oak.

"You're not planning to back through that bog again, are you, mister?" Tupper said.

"No. We're taking the long way around the forest," Fargo said, and saw the relief on the man's face. He had Tupper make a small fire to warm the beef strips, and when the meal was over, he tied the man hand and foot again, took his bedroll down, and stretched out on the opposite side of the embers.

Jennifer came to lie down beside him, moved so that the soft warmth of her thigh rested against him. The gesture was an offering and a concession and he didn't move away. When she turned and came half over him, her breasts softly warm through the nightgown against his skin, he put his arm around her and held her as she went to sleep.

She was still against him when morning came,

and he stirred and watched her pull her eyes open. "Doesn't change anything," he told her gruffly.

"Didn't expect it would," she said, kissed him, and rolled away, scooped the sack up, and went into the trees to dress.

It was when he halted to rest the horses in midafternoon that she came to him while Frank Tupper stretched out on a clump of star moss a half-dozen yards away. "You mind if I ride with him. I'd like to draw him out more," she said. "I think he'll talk to me."

"Even if you don't like what you'll hear?" Fargo asked.

"I'm not afraid of that," she said. "Even if he's right about Eason and the sheriff, that puts a different light on things. Maybe he *is* innocent."

"He's still going back," Fargo growled.

'I know, but maybe I can find out things to help him when we get back," Jennifer insisted.

"Go ahead, talk to him, draw him out all you want," Fargo said. When he mounted up and led the way north around the thick, dark greenery that was the mountain foothills and the surrounding forest land where death had come too close, he rode alone and let Jennifer trot beside Tupper. He shot two jackrabbits before dark fell, and they had enough meat left over for the next day's meal.

Jennifer slept wrapped around him again and he kept Tupper securely bound for the night. The trek around the long expanse of forest land was time-consuming and the days and nights fell into a pattern, Jennifer riding with Tupper a good part of the time, earnestly trying to draw the man out and curling up beside Fargo when night came.

"How you making out with him?" Fargo asked her one night.

"All right, I think," she said. "It takes a while to

gain a person's trust, especially someone in his position."

"We're making good time. You don't have too many days left," he told her.

She nodded and fell silent as she went to sleep.

The next day brought them to good-riding flatland and he kept a steady pace until he drew into an arbor of cottonwoods as dusk descended. He had seen a half-dozen unshod pony trails during the day but none fresh enough to alarm him, and once again he tied Frank Tupper hand and foot.

"You sure don't take chances, do you, Fargo?" the man muttered.

"Works better that way," Fargo said.

"You're going to have me on your conscience, mister," the man said.

"Maybe," Fargo allowed. "I'll wrestle with that when the time comes." He turned away and glimpsed Jennifer going into the trees near where the horses were tethered. He took down his bedroll, undressed, and lay down on it. The fire burned out and a weak moon allowed only the faintest pale light as Jennifer came to lie down beside him. But she didn't curl around him and he turned to see her on one elbow, facing him. "Change of heart?" he remarked.

"I'm just tired of torturing myself," she said. "Let's go off into the woods. You have him all hog-tied."

"Can't risk it," Fargo said. "If he tries to work himself loose, I'll hear it if I'm here. I won't if I'm off in the woods with you."

She lay down and turned her back to him. "Good night," she muttered truculently.

He lay awake until he heard her breathing in the deep rhythm of sleep. The idea of going off with her had certainly appealed to him and he was glad she hadn't used her lips to tempt him further. He closed his eyes and fell asleep but he woke at least four times during the night as Jennifer tossed and turned restlessly.

The first dawn light had spread across the morning sky when he woke again, this time to the cold pressure against the back of his neck. "Don't move, Fargo," he heard Jennifer say from behind him. He stiffened but lay still and felt the cold pressure leave his neck. "Turn around, very slowly," she said.

He obeyed, carefully pulling himself around to see her holding Frank Tupper's gun pointed at him. "When did you get that?" he asked quietly.

"When you were busy tying him up last night. I stopped at your horse and took it out of the saddle-bag," she said.

He looked across to where Frank Tupper was feverishly rubbing his wrist bonds against the rough bark of a tree as he strained and tugged to pull himself free. With no need for stealth, he'd have himself freed in quick enough time, Fargo realized, and he returned his eyes to Jennifer. "This is all wrong, you know," he said quietly. "And it won't work."

"It'll work," she said, and he pushed onto one elbow and heard her voice rise at once. "Don't move. Don't make me shoot."

Fargo eyed the six-gun in her hands, the barrel pointed right at him. She could hardly miss from that range. He decided to stay very still. Her finger on the trigger trembled and nervous tension filled her face. He wasn't convinced she'd shoot, but then he wasn't certain she wouldn't. He was more concerned about making a move that would set off a hair-trigger nervous reaction for which they'd both be sorry, especially him.

A roar of triumph from Tupper broke into his thoughts and he glanced at the man to see that he had shredded the ropes and broken his wrists free. Tupper attacked the ropes binding his ankles and had them off in moments and Fargo flicked a glance at the six-gun still trained on him. Jennifer's nerves were steel-wire tight, he realized. Anything could set her off and he decided to remain still.

Frank Tupper leapt to his feet unfettered by any bonds, ran to the Ovaro, and took the lariat down and strode back where Fargo lay. "Keep that gun on him, honey," Tupper told her as he came around to Fargo's rear, pushed him facedown, and quickly tied his ankles together so that his legs were drawn up behind him. When he finished, he tied Fargo's wrists together in front of him so there was no way the big man could reach the ankle bonds with his hands. "That'll keep him from getting cute," Tupper growled.

Fargo pulled himself up so he could sit on one leg. Jennifer handed Tupper his gun and immediately drew the Colt from Fargo's holster. Tupper walked over to him, pulled the knife from the calf holster around Fargo's leg, and threw it on the ground a dozen feet away.

"I'll see that you have a whole day's start," Jennifer said to the man. "Maybe a lot more."

Tupper nodded, climbed onto the big gray, and sent the horse into a heavy-footed gallop without another glance back. He rode east and turned in to skirt the foothills, Fargo noted before the man was out of sight.

Jennifer sat down a few yards away from where Fargo sat uncomfortably on his left leg. "I'm glad you didn't do anything foolish. I didn't want to have to shoot," she said.

"I'm grateful for small favors," Fargo muttered.

"You're not the only one who does what he has

to do," she said, and he watched the defensiveness touch her face.

"Why'd you do it?"

"He convinced me he's innocent. I don't want to see an innocent man hanged," she said.

"That's not why you did it," Fargo said, and his smile was made of cold chiding. "He convinced you he was innocent but right about everything he said. Letting him run was your way of getting Daddy off the hook."

"That's not so," she shouted, but he saw the tiny circles of color come into her cheeks.

"Tupper hightails it for his life and the hell with going to the marshal. It's all over and done with, and Daddy has no embarrassing questions to answer," Fargo said, and the bitterness came into his voice. "Only what happens to Molly and Amy when I don't come back with him?"

"Nothing. I'll tell them Tupper got away. I'll back you up that you did all you could," she said.

"That's conscience talk. Eason and the sheriff won't buy anything but Frank Tupper," Fargo bit out angrily, and he saw her blink away the flash of uncertainty that had come into her eyes.

"We'll play it out my way from here. It'll all work out, you wait and see," she said with her own grim determination.

Fargo grunted and fell silent. He wondered how much unquestioned faith in Daddy she still had. It didn't matter really, he realized. Loyalty and protectiveness were enough, but he had the suspicion that Frank Tupper had given her more than pause for thought. But she didn't understand men such as Eason and the sheriff. Like rats desperate for survival, they'd stop at nothing, and he couldn't afford to let her combination of protectiveness and naïve stupidity go on.

He waited another half-hour and shifted his weight as she continued to watch him in brooding silence. "I'm real thirsty," he said. "There's water in my canteen." Jennifer rose and went to the Ovaro and returned with the canteen. "You'll have to hold it for me unless you want to untie my hands," he remarked.

"Good try, but no, thanks. I'll hold it for you," she answered as he was certain she would. She put the Colt down, brought the canteen to his lips as she knelt down beside him, tilted it, and he felt the coolness of the water trickle down his throat. He swallowed enough and pulled back and Jennifer brought the canteen down. "Put the lid on tight. It leaks otherwise," he said, and she lowered her eyes to the canteen as she began to screw the cap on.

Fargo's shoulder and neck muscles tightened; he snapped his head around in a whipping motion and felt the top of his head connect with Jennifer's jaw. She went backward and down and he twisted his body to see her sprawled on her back on the ground. She half-raised her head and fell back unconscious.

But she wouldn't stay that way for long, he knew, and he doubled his body almost in two. There was no way he could reach the ropes binding his ankles behind him, but he could reach his double-edged, narrow throwing knife where it lay on the ground. He rolled himself sideways until he reached the knife, grasped it with his fingers, and turned the blade around until he had it against the wrist ropes. Using his fingers only, he began to cut with the knife, each motion a short, sawing one, and he kept one eye on Jennifer as he did. But the blade was razor-sharp, and though his fingers cramped up and he grimaced in pain, he continued to press hard and the wrist ropes parted with surprising quickness. He flung them aside, and with his hands free he could reach the ropes binding his ankles. He had just finished untying the bonds when he heard Jennifer groan and he turned to see her push up on her elbows and shake her head.

She blinked, focused, saw him, and whirled at once as she tried to dive for the Colt on the ground. But Fargo, leaping forward, kicked the gun aside just as her fingers touched the butt. He reached down, yanked her to her feet, and spun her around as she yelped in pain. He dragged her to the Ovaro, took his lariat, and slammed her against the nearest tree. With a half-dozen quick turns he had her strapped to the tree, her arms tight against her sides.

"Damn you, Fargo," she bit out.

"You want to do things the hard way, that's what they'll be," he growled, and finished tying the ropes around her.

"What are you going to do?" she asked.

"Bring Frank Tupper back," Fargo snapped.

"You can't just leave me here," Jennifer protested, alarm coming into her face. "Something could happen to me. You can't afford that."

Fargo smiled. She was hitting where it would do the most good. "You're right," he agreed. "But seeing as how I'll never catch Tupper if I drag you along, I'll have to take that chance." He picked up his things, threw on clothes, and leapt onto the pinto. He raced away and swore silently. There was always the chance that a party of wandering Utes could find her, but he still had no choice but to leave her.

He kept the pinto at a full gallop as he picked up Tupper's trail. The man's heavy horse was no good for long-distance running, he knew, and it wasn't long before he saw Tupper had slowed to a trot. Fargo swerved to his right and climbed into the first row of low hills. There he found a narrow pathway through the trees and kept the Ovaro at a full gallop.

Little more than an hour had gone by when Fargo spotted the big gray below him, moving in and out between trees along an uneven deer trail. He kept the pinto racing along the ridge, glimpsing Tupper below as he passed the man and kept going. He allowed himself another thousand yards before he veered to the left and sent the horse down from the tree-lined ridge.

When he came to the deer trail at the bottom of the hill, he leapt to the ground, pushed the horse into the trees, and pulled the big Sharps from its saddle case. He positioned himself behind a tree at the edge of the trail and only a few minutes passed when Tupper came into sight. Fargo waited, raised the rifle, and took aim. His shot grazed the top of Tupper's head and the man reined up in surprise and alarm. Fargo stepped from behind the tree, the rifle still at his shoulder.

"Get off the horse or the next one's between your eyes," he growled, and Frank Tupper slid to the ground, astonishment on his face. "Throw your gun down," Fargo ordered, and the man obeyed and Fargo lowered the rifle as Tupper stared in disbelief at him. "Don't you just love surprises?" Fargo remarked.

As Tupper backed up at a motion of the rifle, Fargo scooped the gun up, emptied it, and threw it into the trees. He whistled and the Ovaro emerged from the trees and he pulled himself onto the horse. "Mount up," he said. Frank Tupper climbed back onto the wide-backed gray, shocked astonishment still wreathing his face. "Ride, back the way you came," Fargo barked. "I hate to keep a lady waiting."

The man put the big gray into a trot and Fargo

followed a half-pace behind. "You're still making a mistake, Fargo. I'm innocent, I tell you," Tupper said.

"What'd you tell Jennifer that made her buy your story?" Fargo said. "There had to be something more than words."

"Ask her," Tupper grunted.

"'I'll do that," Fargo said, and fell silent.

The sun had just reached the noon sky when he rode up to where Jennifer was still tied to the tree and he felt the rush of relief go through him. She was still his ace-in-the-hole. He saw her eyes take in Frank Tupper with a note of dismay and apology.

Fargo took his lariat and tied Tupper's wrists tight, leaving his hands free to hold the reins. He did the same with Jennifer after he unstrapped her from the tree.

"Is this necessary?" she asked truculently.

"You can answer that yourself, honey," Fargo said. "Let's move." He swung beside Jennifer and led the way westward again, setting a steady pace until night came and he found a spot to bed down. He kept their wrists tied, and when they finished the beef strips, Jennifer rose and tossed him a disdainful glance.

"Untie me so I can get ready for sleep," she said.

"You're ready, just the way you are," he muttered. "Except for one thing more." With a quick motion, he took the lariat, wrapped it around her ankles, and sat her on the ground.

"This is ridiculous," Jennifer snapped.

"You brought it on," he said, and tied Tupper's ankles also. He helped the man to lean against a tree trunk and returned to Jennifer with the blanket. He tossed it down beside her and stretched out on the grass. "You want to tell me what Tupper said to you that convinced you he was innocent?" he asked her.

"I just believed him," she said, but not before he'd caught the moment's hesitation in the answer.

"What the hell's wrong with you?" Fargo snapped. "He thinks I'm one of Eason's hired guns so he won't tell me anything. But you know better. Maybe I can help you, dammit."

"There's nothing," she insisted.

"Hell there isn't," Fargo barked.

Her gray eyes were solemn as they turned to him. "I thought, after our nights together, that you'd care about me, Jennifer Hibbs, the person. But you only care about Jennifer Hibbs the bargaining chip," she said, and managed to sound truly hurt.

"Caring isn't what it's all about. It's about an innocent woman and her little girl," he answered.

"You do what you have to do. I'll do what I have to do," she said, and he swore silently. She'd pulled a wall around herself and whatever Tupper had told her was behind that wall. He broke off further attempts to reach her and concentrated on making time. With the help of a grouse he managed to bring down, they had enough food to see them through the next two days, and he drew to a halt when the terrain grew familiar. Hardrock was but another hour or so ride and he took Tupper and Jennifer up a low hill and into a heavy stand of box elder, had them dismount and strapped each to a tree.

"I'll be coming back for you, that's for sure," he said as he rode away and took their horses with him. The sun had slid into late afternoon when he reached town and he rode to the mayor's house.

Efran Eason flung the door open when he drew to a halt, the man's eyes wide with surprise and uncertainty. "Where's Tupper?" he asked.

"Safe. I brought his horse for now," Fargo said. "You want to make decisions or get your partners?"

"I'll be right back," Eason said, and hurried around the house. He dashed past in a buckboard moments later and Fargo waited quietly beside the fence outside the house.

Sheriff Sideman was first to gallop to a skidding halt, then Eason returned with his buggy, and finally Judge Hibbs on a black mount.

"Where's Jennifer?" the judge barked.

"Keeping Tupper company," Fargo said.

"Abe Tollner and the others?" the sheriff asked.

"They pulled out after a spell," Fargo said.

The sheriff's eyes went to the big, wide-backed gray. "That's Tupper's horse," he said to the judge.

"You get the cigar. You want the horse and Tupper, you bring Molly and the girl," Fargo said.

"Tupper first. Maybe all you have is his horse," Sheriff Sideman said.

Fargo's eyes traveled slowly over the trio, halted on the judge, and stayed there until the man grew uncomfortable.

"What is it, dammit?" Hibbs blurted out.

"Trying to figure how much you love your daughter," Fargo said.

"She's everything to me, damn you," the judge barked.

"Then you'd best make sure your friends don't get cute," Fargo warned. "I'll bring you Tupper for Molly and Amy. I'll still be holding Jennifer, just you remember that."

"There won't be any trouble," Judge Hibbs promised, and Fargo heard the nervous agitation in his voice. He wondered exactly how much leverage the judge could exert on Eason and the sheriff, but he slowly turned the Ovaro and led the other two horses with him.

"Wait here," he said. "With Molly and the girl." He put the horses into a trot and rode away as dusk began to turn into night. He made his way back along the road that led from the town, turned up into the low hills, and approached the thick stand of box elder from the side. Only the faintest touch of moonlight penetrated the thick foliage as he found where he'd left Tupper and Jennifer. He unstrapped the man from the tree but kept his wrists tied. "I'll be taking you in now," he said to Tupper, who shrugged in resignation.

"You're leaving me here?" Jennifer frowned.

"With a gag around your mouth. Can't have you screaming for help. Somebody just might hear you," Fargo said.

"What if?" she asked, her gray eyes wide as they peered gravely at him.

"What if they didn't keep their word about Molly?" Fargo finished for her, and she nodded, her face tight.

"And if they kill you," she murmured.

"Then we'll both be sorry," he said as he put the kerchief around her mouth and drew it tight. He turned away from the pain and accusing in the gray eyes, swung onto the Ovaro, and led Tupper through the thick trees on the heavy gray. He rode beside Tupper, his hand resting on the butt of the Colt in its holster in case Tupper should try a last-minute, desperate attempt to run. But the man rode silently beside him, and as he neared the end of town, he steered the horses to Efran Eason's house.

The trio rushed outside as he came to a halt and then a fourth figure followed and he took in Olson's burly form. Fargo drew the Colt and fastened it on Olson as he spoke to the others. "Where's Molly and the girl?" he growled .

"Perfectly safe," Judge Hibbs said quickly. "There

152

wasn't time to get her here. Olson will take you to her. Everything's in order, Fargo. I wouldn't risk Jennifer, dammit."

"Meantime we'll just take Mr. Frank Tupper to a nice cell," Sideman said, and pulled Tupper from the gray.

Efran Eason came to Tupper's other side and pushed a six-gun into the man's ribs. "Start walking," he growled, and Tupper began to shuffle forward with Eason and the sheriff flanking him.

Fargo felt the uneasiness curling inside him. He flashed a glance at Judge Hibbs as the man fell in just behind Eason and his prisoner. He seemed to be more anxious than nervous, and he turned to Fargo. "How do I get Jennifer?" he questioned.

"I'll deliver her to your place soon as I have Molly and the girl," Fargo said and the judge nodded and hurried after Eason and the sheriff.

Olson stepped to the side of the house and returned on a dark-brown horse.

"Let's go," the man said, and Fargo fell in beside him. Olson's heavy, mean face stayed impassive as he led the way around town and continued south. It was going too smoothly, Fargo knew. They had to play it out, he knew. But it was equally plain that they couldn't let Molly and Amy stay alive. They knew too much now. Not specifics but more than enough to tell others what had happened, and the questions would gather quickly. But Molly and Amy were still alive, he was certain of that. They had to keep them alive in case he had demanded to see them. But Olson wasn't taking him to Molly so he could ride off with her, Fargo muttered silently.

"How much farther?" he asked after they'd been a half-hour out of town to the north.

"Another mile or so," Olson answered.

Fargo smiled inwardly and decided to pull a little more proof out to satisfy himself. "I'm glad nobody did anything stupid," he commented. "But then I didn't ever figure the judge would risk his daughter's neck." Olson rode in silence. "I'd guess Hibbs carries more weight than anyone else," Fargo said.

"You can always buy a new judge," Olson said.

"But the judge cares about his daughter," Fargo pressed.

"That doesn't mean anyone else gives a damn," Olson said as they came in sight of a shack where the glow of lamplight probed into the night.

Fargo felt the grimness stabbing at him. He'd heard enough. Eason and Sideman would sacrifice Hibbs as well as Jennifer if they had to. Molly and Amy had been already written off.

"I've still got a score to settle with you, Fargo," Olson rasped.

Fargo shrugged and slowly lifted the Colt from its holster, turned it so he held the gun by the barrel. He wanted no shots to alert whoever was inside with Molly. He slowed the pinto ever so slightly to drop back half a pace and his arm came up and down with all his strength in a short, chopping blow. The butt of the gun struck Olson alongside the side of his head, and with a half-grunt, the man's burly form toppled from the horse.

Fargo leapt to the ground and saw, in surprise, Olson came on his feet shaking his head. Fargo sent a whistling left that smashed into the man's jaw and Olson's burly figure staggered backward, swayed, and Fargo's right smashed into the same spot. Olson went down and lay still. Fargo took his gun and threw it into the darkness and vaulted onto the pinto again. He sent the horse toward the cabin and halted when he was but a few yards from what turned out to be a ramshackle shack with a window at the nearest side.

He crawled to the window sill and carefully peered into the single room. Molly, Amy beside her, sat on the floor in one corner and two men lounged across from them. A low fire burned in a small fireplace and Fargo saw the remains of a chicken that had been cooked on an iron skillet. He unholstered the Colt once more and crept noiselessly to the door, gathered himself, and crashed the door open with one shoulder.

The two men leapt up in surprise, reached for their guns, but Fargo fired, one shot then a half-spin for the second, and neither man had cleared his holster as they fell and landed almost with their heads touching.

Molly was in his arms instantly, Amy beside her, clinging and hugging with half-sobs of relief. "Oh, good God, it's over. It's over," Molly breathed.

"For you," he said. "I've a few loose ends to wrap up. They treat you all right?"

"Good enough, I guess, but it was the waiting and wondering if each day might be our last," Molly said.

"I'll take you home," Fargo said, and led her outside. He used one of the horses tied in the back for Molly and let Amy ride the other one, and when he neared Hardrock, he approached Molly's place without passing through town.

"Home," Molly breathed. "What a wonderful word."

He started to leave and she clutched at him at once. "I'll be back," he told her reassuringly, and she finally let him go. He rode at a fast canter through the night and hurried to the thick stand of box elder, where he saw Jennifer's head lift as she

155

heard him coming. He dismounted, took the gag from her, and untied her completely.

"I take it Molly and the little girl were safe and sound," she said with an edge to her voice.

"Be glad for it," Fargo muttered.

"I am," she said with a rush of sincerity.

"That makes two of us," Fargo agreed, and she climbed onto the filly and followed him down the hill. "I told the judge I'd deliver you home," he said as they came in sight of town.

"I'd rather go by myself," she said stiffly. "You've done quite enough for me, thank you."

"You could say that," he answered mildly, and drew a quick glare.

She sent the horse into a canter and rode away, and Fargo smiled after her, then turned the Ovaro and followed her into town. He rode slowly, let her disappear from sight, and when he reached town, he rode to the jail and dismounted.

The front office was dark and the shade drawn on the door, but he caught the faint flickering light of a candle burning somewhere inside. He tried the door and found it locked and felt the frown of surprise on his face. He'd expected they'd been spending more time with Frank Tupper and he tried the door again and knocked. No one answered and a sudden stab of apprehension speared into him. He lifted his leg and kicked out with all his strength and the door flew open.

He pushed into the jail and saw the flickering candle inside the cell. He also saw Frank Tupper's figure, stripped to the waist, lying across a cot. Trickles of blood ran down the man's face and Fargo saw the burn marks on his skin. A curse escaped him as he ran into the cell. Tupper managed to open one eye that had not been battered shut. "What happened?" Fargo barked.

"They made me tell," Tupper breathed.

"Tell what?" Fargo asked.

"Where I hid everything," Tupper managed. "All the checks, records, all the evidence against them."

"Where is it?" Fargo pressed, and the man's eye closed. Fargo shook him gently and Tupper pulled his eye open again.

"Old grain shed, just outside town," the man gasped. "Hid everything there, right under their noses."

Fargo's frown dug into his forehead. "Is this what you told Jennifer?" he asked. "Is this what made her sure you were innocent?"

Tupper managed to nod. "Told her," he breathed. "Told her."

"Goddamn," Fargo bit out as he pushed to his feet and raced from the jail. He knew now why Jennifer had wanted to go home by herself. She'd another stop to make first. She wanted to see that evidence Tupper had told her about with her own eyes before confronting her father. Only now Eason and the sheriff were on their way there. Maybe they were there already, Fargo grimaced as he vaulted onto the pinto and raced through the night streets of Hardrock. He had noticed the old grain shed just outside the north end of town, and he sent the horse galloping through Hardrock and out of town and slowed to a halt when he spied the long shed. He leapt to the ground, the Colt in his hand, and raced in a crouch toward the shed.

A side door hung half from its hinges and he crept inside, saw the glow of lamplight from the far end, and hurried forward on silent steps. He stayed behind a row of boxes and barrels and saw the figures come into view. Jennifer stood with a ledger in one hand, a shuffle of papers half out of a file box in front of her. The judge held one hand on her arm and Fargo saw Sideman and the mayor across from them. The sheriff had his gun pointed at Jennifer. "You can't do this," Fargo heard Hibbs say.

"We got to do it," Sideman said. "We'll get us a new judge."

"You won't get away with it. People will ask what happened to me and to Jennifer if we just disappear," the man said.

"You were suddenly called back East on family matters," Efran Eason said, a note of triumph in his toadlike face.

"Fargo will come asking for me," Jennifer said. "I know he will."

The sheriff laughed. "Fargo's dead by now," he said.

"He isn't. He came back and let me go," Jennifer answered.

"Good try, my dear," Eason said.

"It's not polite to doubt a lady's word," Fargo said softly, and saw Eason and Sideman whirl. The sheriff fired at once, two shots in the direction his voice had come. The first splintered a crate to his right, the second came closer. Fargo fired back and the man's shifty eyes suddenly grew large as his chest exploded in a shower of red. He flew backward into a pile of old boxes and crashed lifelessly to the floor.

Efran Eason was darting for safety, trying to race down a passage between two rows of old crates. Fargo ran between two barrels and reached the passage as Eason came along. He lifted a whistling left hook and Eason went into the air, flew against a barrel, and Fargo's right followed, crashed into the man's jaw. Eason spun, hurtling into a pile of old crates. Fargo heard the man's gargled scream of pain.

He ran forward and saw the mayor's short form

sprawled facedown. A sharp sliver of wood from one of the old crates protruded from between his shoulder blades. He resembled a doll discarded because it was old and misshapen.

Fargo holstered the Colt and stepped back to where Jennifer waited with her father, the man's silver hair suddenly straggly, his usually imperious eyes hollow.

"I told you this town's going to need a new sheriff and a new mayor," he said. "Where's all the money you three stole?"

"It's in a special account," Hibbs said.

"There's a town council, I take it," Fargo said, and the judge nodded.

"Make your peace with them. Give it all back and maybe they'll let you go your way without anything more," Fargo said.

"He'll do that. I promise," Jennifer said.

Fargo turned and started to walk from the old shed and halted at the door as he heard Jennifer hurrying after him. Her gray eyes held his as she put a hand on his arm.

"Maybe you have done a lot for me," she murmured. "It's not all happy, but I won't be forgetting any of it."

"Especially some parts?" He smiled.

"Especially some parts." She nodded and her lips paused on his, a soft reminder, and he knew he'd not be forgetting so quickly.

He left her as she turned back into the old shed and he rode back through town, drew to a halt at Molly's place.

She opened the door for him. "Amy's fast asleep," Molly said. "Probably the first sound sleep she's had in too long." She closed the door and let the robe she wore fall open.

159

"I'd say it's time to take up where we left off," Fargo said.

"Exactly what I'd say," Molly agreed, and took him in her arms.

Later, as Molly lay beside him, satisfied and satiated, Fargo wondered who he'd be remembering most in the months to come; warm, sweet Molly, fiercely independent, sinuous Jennifer, or the strange wild dark catlike creature of the dead man's forest.

LOOKING FORWARD!

**The following is the opening
section from the next novel in the exciting
Trailsman series from Signet:**

THE TRAILSMAN #84
UTAH SLAUGHTER

*1860, Utah Territory, home of
the Latter-Day Saints. From the
Great Salt Lake to desolate rimrock canyons
where religious fury can save a man's
soul or help him lose his life. . . .*

The big Ovaro's ears perked up and tension altered his easy walk. The slight change in his gait was imperceptible to anyone except the tall man in the custom saddle.

If Skye Fargo had been able to twitch his ears, he would have, if only to persuade some of the buzzing flies to land somewhere else. As it was, he shook his shoulder-length black hair. Extending his muscular legs, he stood straight in the stirrups. He twisted his broad hat brim lower to discourage the noontime sun. His lake-blue eyes squinted to the south, across the sagebrush and bunchgrass.

That seemed to be where those disturbing sounds had come from, but he scanned all around, just to be sure. The ground nearby was just dry, rolling prairie, broken by ravines and sporadic buttes, but distant blue-tinged mountains shimmered in every direction.

The sounds rang out again. The dull reports came from the south, almost dead ahead. Most likely just hunters fetching meat for a wagon train on the Oregon Trail.

Fargo checked his mental map. He was somewhere between the Bear River and Ham's Fork of the Green. The Oregon Trail still had to be at least twenty, and maybe forty, miles farther south. So many folks were heading west these days, though game was mighty sparse anywhere near the trail. A hunter might have to venture this far if he wanted to return to camp with anything much bigger than a jackrabbit.

The Trailsman started to swear to himself again, but caught himself. He wanted to make sure he was hearing what he didn't want to hear. Besides the dull reports of guns, there were shrill war whoops. Sure, there were hunters up there—Indians hunting two-legged game. Now that he knew where to look, he could make out puffs of powder smoke rising then dissipating into the calm air. All this was beyond a few rises and dips, not more than five miles away.

He really didn't need to prod the Ovaro toward the unseen action, but he did. While the husky horse pounded across a draw and started uphill, the Trailsman checked his weapons.

The Sharps carbine, secure although bouncing in its canvas saddle boot, sat right at hind. The grips of his heavy Army-model Colt revolver, holstered on his right hip, poked at his lean abdomen every now and again, as did the half of the big knife he kept on the other side of his belt. Down by his right foot, the razor-edged throwing knife didn't seem likely to slip out of the leather sheath that was sewn inside the bootleg.

In open country, riding in over a ridge was a sure way to get yourself killed, giving somebody an easy skyline shot. The Trailsman reined up and took the last hundred yards on foot, his Sharps in hand.

A mile of the gulch that spread before him was occupied by traveling pilgrims. If they had any live-stock or real wagons, though, he sure as hell couldn't see them. They had about fifty two-wheeled wooden carts that they'd been pushing and pulling them-selves. As a dozen short and squat Bannock braves were charging up and down the sides of the gulch on their paint ponies, the womenfolk and children were trying to hide under the carts. Men crouched next to a few of the carts, firing sporadically and ineffectively at the Indians.

Any minute now, the band of Bannocks would get serious about the raid. Already some were shoot-ing arrows, and one had found its mark. A shaft stuck out of a bearded man's shoulder. Too pain-stricken to be sensible and get back under the cart, he was crawling toward a clump of brush, dragging his old muzzle-loader through the grit.

A nearby brave caught the motion, dismounted with a leap, and headed over to intercept the pil-grim and add his scalp to the three that already dangled from his coup-stick.

As good a place to start as any, Fargo figured. From his prone position, he got the brave in his sights and exhaled slowly as he squeezed the trigger of his Sharps. The .50-caliber bullet caught the skulk-ing warrior square in his bare chest, slamming him back as the force straightened him from his crouch.

He began to spin and fall, but the Trailsman didn't have time to watch.

He could expect maybe thirty seconds of reasonably easy shooting before the Indians would be able to respond to his presence. That meant four shots if all went well, and he intended to make the most of the opportunity. His nimble fingers jammed another paper cartridge into the Sharps' breech. He instinctively snapped the lever to bring up the block, then thumbed another percussion cap onto the nipple.

Two Bannocks swinging war clubs rode straight for the women and children huddled under several carts. The Trailsman adjusted his aim and caught the lead warrior in one shoulder. Blood, sinew, and bone fragments sprayed outward, right into the next horse's muzzle. The pony reared in fright, so suddenly that Fargo's next bullet hit lower than anticipated.

He'd aimed for a chest shot, but the slug caught the Bannock in the center of his loincloth. The blood erupted like a geyser, and if the falling brave lived, it was a safe bet that he'd fathered his last child.

Hearing noises to the right, Fargo swung the Sharps. Now the Indians knew he was there and up to no good, at least as far as they were concerned. Four braves, low on their horses, galloped his way in a twisting single file. Fargo aimed at the lead rider, hoping to punch a half-inch hole in his gaudy hide shield. Something deflected the slug which grazed the warrior's side, leaving a crimson slash, painful, maybe, but not enough to put the warrior out of action. And they were still coming.

Didn't those pilgrims down there believe in helping out somebody that was helping them?

From the corner of his eye, Fargo saw they still

had their hands full, although most of the remaining Bannocks were headed up the swell and starting to converge on him.

The Sharps pierced the second rider in the neck, almost tearing the man's sullen head off as the soft lead slammed into his neck bones and expanded. The gape-mouthed rider, eyes going blank, stayed atop his charging mount for several paces before slumping back, to slide and tumble down the horse's rump.

Damn. Two more were coming up dead ahead, no more than fifty yards off. The hot barrel of the quick-swung Sharps barked twice. A pair of bleeding Bannocks were dead, both from head shots, before hitting the sagebrush.

The group on the right was almost within coup-stick range now, no more than fifteen or twenty yards off. Moving too fast for the Sharps, the brave in back with a short horn bow sent an arrow past Fargo's ear.

Damn it, why hadn't he thought to fort up better before starting to shoot? No time, that's why. And why wasn't he getting any cover from those folks down below? A few shots from those handcarts, and these Bannock would vanish like beer on payday.

Too close and dodging too fast for the carbine now, Fargo rolled and pulled his Colt while it started to rain arrows all around him. Sprawled on his belly, he sure as hell couldn't keep those shafts out of his back.

Fargo hoped the Ovaro had sense enough to run off before these bastards added him to their herd of stolen horseflesh. The Trailsman used a precious bullet to take down the closest Indian pony. The carcass would give him something to hunker behind, so his back wouldn't become a pincushion. He nailed the hammer-headed pony, the nearest one, square between its eyes. Before collapsing, the mare reflexively pounded several steps toward the craw-fishing Trailsman. The rider began to leap off his dead mount, springing toward Fargo swinging his stone-tipped club.

Fargo ducked the swing and brought his head up, slamming it into the warrior's jaw. That brain-jolting bump should have knocked the bastard cold, but the sweaty brave twisted and jammed a knee into Fargo's balls.

The Trailsman winced and slammed his Colt's barrel into his opponent's heaving ribs, swinging round so that he had the dead horse behind him and the brave in front, lessening the chance that some archer would get lucky with an arrow.

The warrior almost shattered Fargo's arm with the club and the gun fell. Trying for a bearhug, Fargo grabbed the Bannock, then rolled back against the horse's midriff. The shrill whoops and deep grunts of the other warriors kept getting louder. He and the writhing warrior grappled amid several cir-cling horsemen who'd lost interest in the handcart caravan now that there was a more entertaining fight up here.

His left hip was pinned to the ground, so there wasn't any way to reach the belt knife. If it wasn't impossible to push his pain-fired arm down to his right boot for the throwing knife, then it was damn close. He'd have to release the bearhug, which would give the redskin a chance to sit up and swing that club. The foul-breathed Bannock carried a metal scalping knife, in a beaded scabbard on a rawhide sling. Without worrying about whether his desper-ate plan would work, Fargo snapped off the bearhug.

As the surprised warrior sprang upward, the Trailsman's big hand threw a fistful of grit into the round-faced Bannock's eyes.

The astonished warrior blinked and pawed, giving Fargo just enough time to grab the knife before the brave caught on. The next thing the Bannock noticed—and the last thing he noticed—was the dull edge sawing into his throat. A geyser of blood sprayed forward, momentarily blinding the Trailsman as he forced the blade to continue its savage progress through the man's windpipe, tendon by tough tendon until the man's motions were nothing more than the reflexive spasms of sudden death.

Fargo rolled his blood-spurting burden away. At least one thing went right. The body sprawled between the dead horse's front and hind legs, leaving a small square where he had some protection against the arrows that would start flying any second.

The Indians would likely give up by nightfall, but the blinding sun still sat high in the sky. He found the Colt easily enough, but the Sharps sat just outside his corpse-walled fort. Reaching for it was like asking somebody to kill him. All the six remaining Bannocks had to do was wait around, just out of effective pistol range, sending in arrows every now and again. Then sometime this afternoon, he too would be finding out whether the Happy Hunting Ground was a real place, or just some story. Unless he got some help from that worthless caravan down in the draw. Fargo hunkered against the dead horse's belly, disturbing the buzzing flies that had materialized from nowhere, wiped the sweat and blood out of his eyes with his flannel sleeve, and wondered whether it was worth peeking down that way. The handcart brigade would doubtless move on long before the Indians would. For all he could tell, they were trudging along right at this moment.

Who the hell were they, anyway? Every now and again, some down-on-his-luck Missouri greenhorn, unable to afford a wagon and oxen, would venture west with a handcart and hope to find his fortune. But a whole train of carts? With dozens of women and children, only a handful of men?

Wait a minute. The Mormons down in Great Salt Lake City were sending missionaries all over the world these days. The Latter-Day Saints were supposed to emigrate to their Zion in Utah Territory. But a lot of their new converts didn't have two nickels to rub together, and sometimes the best the church could do for them was rig them up with handcarts and organize a caravan.

The Trailsman cared little about their religious beliefs, but as a sometime wagonmaster, he respected the sensible way they traversed the wilderness between Missouri and the Great Salt Lake. Mormon trains were disciplined and organized, led by experienced men who knew their business.

Families and handcarts—had to be Mormon emigrants. But without any supply wagons to tote the heavy stuff and the folks who got sick? Getting all strung out so that they couldn't bunch up for protection when they were in hostile Indian country? And heading the wrong way? If they kept going up this gulch, then went up the Bear instead of down it, they'd end up deep in Shoshoni country with about two hundred miles of rugged mountains and mean deserts between them and their earthly utopia.

Fargo peeked out, and got only a glimpse before an arrow thudded into the dead pony's neck, just inches from where his head had been. As he figured, the surviving Indians were paired up in various directions, sitting out there on their rough saddles while they stared intently at his enclosure. They could afford to be patient. He was getting thirsty, his stomach was growling, and his canteen and traveling grub were aboard the Ovaro.

"Next time," Fargo told himself, "you stop to help some folks, make sure they're folks that'll help you. This is just plain foolish, sitting here in the flies and sunshine, holding a Colt with four rounds that won't do you a lick of good against those Bannocks out there."

There weren't many Bannocks these days, since the tribe had been almost wiped out by smallpox a few years back. The survivors seemed to take it personally. They believed that the white men had deliberately introduced the lethal disease as a faster and easier way to kill off the red men along the Oregon Trail. Usually the Bannock rode father north, where they had an off-and-on truce with the Shoshoni. But they were here now, and making godawful nuisances of themselves.

Fargo figured he didn't have much choice but to wait them out. Once darkness settled, he could leave his tiny fort easily enough. But then he'd be afoot in hostile Indian country, unless the Ovaro somehow found him. He guessed he'd just have to worry about that when the time came. Right now he was thirsty, so parched that if the feeling got any worse, he'd jab the dead horse, catch some blood in his hat, and convince himself that it tasted good.

Sleep seemed like a painless way to pass time until darkness. But it would be just his luck that the Bannock would try one more charge before sunset, and if he didn't wake in time, they'd be waving his scalp at tonight's party. So he'd have to stay alert.

Boom.

What the hell was that? Sounded like a baby cannon in the vast sun-drenched stillness. Colt at ready, Fargo shifted and peeked toward the explosion. There was a cloud and scurrying in a clump of sagebrush behind where one Indian, his slimy intestines tumbling out of a huge hole where his belly had just been, was pitching forward on a horse that suddenly wanted to be somewhere else.

His partner whirled in his saddle, just in time to catch a full load of buckshot. Fur-clad braids flew apart as his head dissolved in a cloud of rose-hued mist. Gratified that somebody from the handcart caravan had enough gumption to sneak up here and help him out, Fargo saw the pair on his right kick their mounts toward their fallen comrades.

Instead of circling, they unthinkingly rode straight, which brought them within range of his Colt. Steadying the butt on the dead horse's flank, he plunked the closer one in the shoulder and sent a bullet into the second one's chest. They lost further interest in today's battle. The other pair of Indians started sending arrows his way while they took the long way around. They figured on picking up the two wounded braves and heading on back to camp, since the party was over.

Fargo would have preferred to end their careers right then and there, but he had only two rounds left in the Colt, and they were moving too fast. And it only seemed reasonable to wait until they departed before leaving his cadaverous fort to fetch his Sharps.

The Trailsman got within steps of the big sagebrush clump before the gent who'd helped him stood up. Clad in dust-caked bib overalls and sporting a battered hat with a monstrous brim, he didn't look up at Fargo, although he needed to—the crown of the hat barely reached Fargo's shoulder. Maybe he was just a boy; his small size must have helped him sneak up here while the Bannocks had their eyes on Fargo. His callused but tiny hands gripped a double-barrelled shotgun, pointed toward his tattered shoes.

"I'm obliged, sir," the Trailsman finally said. "Must have taken considerable effort to work your way up here close enough to use that scattergun."

"You needn't call me sir," the soft voice answered, still not looking up.

So he was just a boy, then. People could be awful formal about who got to be called sir. "Hell, whether you're a sir or not, I'm still damn grateful you decided to take a hand in this. Those redskins had me pinned down pretty tight."

"It is we who should be grateful to you, sir, for coming to our aid when we were attacked." The smooth-voiced boy finally looked up at the Trailsman, who blinked at least twice.

Either this boy had an awfully soft and round face, or Skye Fargo was looking into the dark eyes of a woman who'd just crawled away from her caravan and killed two Indians at close range with a shotgun. Maybe he should have guessed that earlier, but those baggy overalls obscured any figure she might have.

Fargo swept off his hat and bowed a bit. "I'm Skye Fargo, ma'am."

Her eyes brightened in the shadow of the hat. "Branwen Gwynedd," she announced in not much more than a whisper. "Would you be the man we heard about back at Fort Laramie? The Trailsman?"

"Been called worse," Fargo replied. "I'd guess you're not long from Wales."

"My parents came from Wales," she nodded, "but I was born in Ohio." Branwen pointed toward the caravan. Folks were starting to crawl out from under their carts, and those on their feet were staring at him and Branwen. "I must return," she whispered. "We are not to have any intercourse with the Gentiles." She turned and began to trudge down the hillside.

Fargo legged along behind her, although he swung toward the carts in the lead. So he was a Gentile? Then they had to be Mormons. But this was the most miserable excuse for an emigrant caravan he'd ever seen. The Saints never ran something in such a haphazard, stupid way. He best have a word or two with whoever was in charge.

It wasn't any wonder that they hadn't given him more help. Nobody in this caravan looked fit to do much more than sleep. Well, most of the kids looked okay, since they just walked along most days. But the women, most of them were as small as Branwen. Clad in severe gray homespun, they appeared gaunt and dazed. There were only half a dozen men among the seventy or so people, and they too were thin as broomsticks, their eyes vacant and almost glazed.

That happens, Fargo mused, when you turn human beings into draft animals. And when he asked "Who's in charge here?" the cluster of men just stood there, looking at their feet and each other.

"Look, gents, I'm not here to do you any harm. I just need to talk to your captain. Now, can somebody point me to him?"

They gestured toward the rear. Fargo couldn't make out the words, but he could tell that a black-clad man atop a roan was saying something to Branwen, who stood next to her cart. As the Trailsman stepped that way, along the row of carts and the sagging, tired emigrants, the man's tirade became distinct.

"Shameful enough it is, Sister Branwen, that you affect the garb of men, despite the teachings of our church. And then today you left the train, despite my orders that all were to stay with their carts, no matter what transpired. They tell me you raised your hand against a Lamanite. With my own eyes, I saw you speak to a heathen."

She looked up to say something, but the man in the saddle cut her off. "There is no excuse, Sister Branwen, no excuse whatsoever for your transgressions."

Branwen hesitantly turned her head toward the Trailsman, who was almost at her side. The mounted man had a surprisingly lean face under his close-trimmed dark beard. It bristled after he caught Branwen's motion and spun to glare at Fargo. "Who are you, heathen?" he demanded. Fargo answered and asked pretty much the same question.

"Alexander Newman, divinely anointed captain of this party of emigrants." The mounted man seemed to savor that distinction, because he paused for a bit, his brown eyes aimed down at Fargo. "You were the one on the ridge?"

"That's where I was," Fargo allowed as his temper rose. "And where the hell were you, Newman? Hiding down here under some of these long skirts?"

Newman grimaced. "You mind your own business, Gentile."

"My business is what I make it, Newman. What's yours?"

Newman looked perplexed for a moment before he recalled his business. "To lead the Host of Israel to Zion. That's my business, heathen."

"I'd say your business is slow, cold-blooded murder, Newman."

"How dare you say that." Newman shifted the reins from his right hand to his left. His right moved toward one of the big pistols that hung Texas-style from holsters that flanked his saddle-horn. Perhaps to distract Fargo's attention, he launched an explanation.

"My business is leading this caravan of handcarts." Newman's voice quavered and cracked a bit, but he went on. "Our first leader, Captain Watson, was unfortunately drowned when we forded the Green."

"The Green does run high this time of year," Fargo prodded, keeping his eyes on Newman's right arm. The man's hand had dipped below the saddle, so Fargo couldn't see it. But if the arm moved forward, it would mean the man was reaching for his pistol. Fargo would be ready.

"So we gathered to pray for guidance, and cast lots to see who should lead the party," Newman continued. "I was anointed."

"And you've been in charge ever since?" Fargo provoked.

Newman answered with a nod.

"What happened to your supply wagons? I reckon you'd have to have a few, even if most folks are using handcarts. There's food to haul, and those emigrants that get sick or hurt could ride in the wagons till they got well. But where are your wagons, Newman?"

Newman glared and hissed sharply as he inhaled.

His right arm moved forward a bit, but not enough. "We had to abandon the wagons when the Lamanites stampeded our stock," he confessed.

"And you were the leader, right? Did you set up camp with your carts in a square and put your stock inside the square, so that the Indians couldn't stampede your critters?"

Newman shrugged. "I didn't know."

"The hell you didn't. If you got this far, your late Captain Watson must have done it the right way. I'll bet he didn't let you get all strung out in a single file in Indian country, either, so that you couldn't fort up in a hurry if you needed to. Weren't you paying any attention, Newman?"

"But. . . ." Newman began to protest.

Fargo ignored the man's attempted interruption and continued. The Trailsman's temper now provided his words.

"Look, Newman. You did know better than to run a caravan like this. Maybe you didn't know better than to swing north when you should have been heading south, though I doubt that. And if you're the leader, it's your job to lead when you get attacked, not ride off and hide somewhere. Way I see it, you were trying to get everybody here killed, one way or another."

"Heathen, you've just called me a coward and a murderer," Newman spat. His right arm lunged forward.

The Trailsman's Colt came up and barked. Blood sprayed from Newman's wounded forearm. He jerked it up, dropping the pistol he had intended to bring round. His roan reared as Fargo stepped back, Colt still ready.

Newman jerked the reins with his left hand, momentarily calming his mount. He looked around and saw nothing that looked like a friendly face. He relaxed the reins. The edgy roan bounded up the side of the draw, bearing Newman away in silence.

The tense silence reigned until Branwen spoke up. "Mr. Fargo, who's to lead us now?"

Without a leader, these pilgrims would have trouble finding a river from an island, and their leader had just high-tailed it to points unknown. The misled emigrants were forty miles off their rightful path, and in Bannock and Shoshoni country at that. Fargo had places to go—but to just ride off now would be to condemn these people to death.

Hating what he had to say, Fargo turned to Branwen. "Looks like I've got the job unless somebody else wants it."

There weren't any volunteers.